Bandy

Craig R. Hipkins

Published by: Hipkins Twins

Bandy

Copyright ©2024 Craig R. Hipkins

www.hipkinstwins.com

Print ISBN: 979-8-9858196-6-3

Library of Congress Control Number: Pending

Thanks & Dedication

I would like to dedicate this book to anyone who has suffered from oppression and cruelty.

I would like to thank my editors and proofreaders who took the time to read this book and offer me advice and encouragement.

Cover Art by: Duy Phan

Chapter 1

I t was a crimson dusk. Wispy ribbons of gray, white, and pink had settled in the western sky. It had a tranquilizing effect on the young boy sitting in silent contemplation on a flat rock overlooking a placid pond. His tired eyes scanned the elongated body of water. Thick autumn foliage draped the shoreline. It was quiet here. That was the way he liked it. The only sounds came from nature. A croaking frog, crickets chirping, or a whip-poor-will hiding in the bushes were normal sounds.

Occasionally, the boy would add to the din. A loud discharge would issue from his throat. It was a sort of birdcall, not unlike that of a mourning dove, but unique. It was his own savage call to nature. It was a wild, singular cry that penetrated the dusk and conjoined his being with the feral creatures of the woods.

He knew them all and they knew him. His father had brought him here to fish when he was small. He had been coming back here ever since. He was still only a stripling of thirteen, but he felt much older. In fact, since his father's illness, he had been forced, out of necessity, to step into his shoes. He was the oldest boy and his younger siblings looked up to him for guidance and support.

1

He picked up a smooth oval rock and threw it. He watched it skim across the water, creating small ripples. It was autumn. The nights were getting colder. A slight breeze wafted through the trees. The boy wrapped his long thin arms around his knees and watched a crisp yellow maple leaf skip across the smooth surface of the rock, twisting and turning with the irregular movement of the wind. For a brief second it stopped in front of him, as if it might be saying *hello*. It was then lifted by a terrific gust and, joined by hundreds of its companions, hurried across the lake like an attacking army.

"Acer rubrum," mumbled the boy, practicing his Latin.

"You don't say," came a hollow, somewhat piping voice from the trees behind him.

The boy craned his neck around and surveyed the tree line from where he thought the voice had originated. There, sitting on the loping branch of a fine specimen of Acer rubrum was a passenger pigeon. The boy cracked a smile, showing his gleaming white teeth. He waved. The branch bobbled slightly when the bird took flight and with a smooth glide, alighted on the boy's shoulder and pecked softly at his ear.

"Why so glum, young Isaac?" the pigeon asked.

Isaac shook his head and with the snap of his forefinger, he playfully tapped the pink belly of his friend. His name was Bandy because of the distinctive feathered black band around his neck. This distinct marking was not typical of a passenger pigeon. Isaac could easily identify him by it. Not that he needed any help in that sense, since as far as he knew, Bandy was the only pigeon that could talk.

"I am not glum, Bandy. What makes you think so?"

The boy swept his long flaxen hair away from his eyes as Bandy fluttered away from his shoulder and landed on his left knee.

Bandy was an exquisite example of a passenger pigeon. The bluish head and pale-gray wings sprinkled with homely black spots only differed from the norm by the enigma of the band.

"Keehoo! Keehoo!"

Isaac rolled his eyes. "Oh, don't go keehooing me, Bandy. I am not in any mood to be keehooed today!"

Bandy flapped his wings and cocked his head to the side. "So, you are glum! I knew it. I always know when you are glum—or happy. I can sense it!"

The boy buried his head in his arms, all the while tapping his fingers on his elbows. "My father is sick. I do not think he shall last much longer, Bandy," he replied. When he finally raised his head, Bandy could see a tear falling down his cheek.

A stiff silence followed until the bird flew back onto Isaac's shoulder. "This news... It pains me to hear it, young Isaac. I am all too familiar with the loss of a parent. I watched in horror as a vile hunter shot my mother and father out of the sky with a single blast of one of those murderous scatter-guns!"

An uncomfortable silence followed. Isaac busied himself by twirling the stem of a leaf between his thumb and finger. Bandy was watching him with concern. He had seen his friend unhappy before, but nothing like this. He was worried. He flapped his wings and began circling around Isaac's head trying to cheer him up.

"Don't be sad, Isaac. I don't like it when you are sad," Bandy said.

The boy frowned and let his gaze wander across the pond. He could hear the distant sound of a factory steam whistle and knew that his mother would be coming home. He adjusted the

4

collar on his wool coat. It was going to be a cold night.

Bandy finally alighted on Isaac's shoulder again and carefully nudged his earlobe with his beak. "Stay strong, young Isaac. Your family needs you. You must remain solid and tough, and persevere," Bandy piped.

Isaac ignored his feathered friend. He merely sat there twirling the leaf before flicking it onto the rock and watching the wind whisk it away.

He now found himself at a crossroads in his life. With his father nearing death, he would soon be forced to quit school and go to work in the mills. His dream of becoming a scholar would be squashed forever. It was now all too obvious to him. His future would be a bleak one. It would be a life of constant toil, working long days in the mills to support his mother and younger siblings. His father had done his best for him. He had labored in the mills as well as the fields. It had been brutal work that had gradually worn him down, but he had managed to scrape up enough money to buy his oldest son books. He had known Isaac was different. He was not like other boys. He was quiet and bookish. Sure, he enjoyed fishing and tramping through the woods, but he needed his time to read...and learn.

Bandy gave him a peck on the cheek.

"Keehoo! Keehoo!"

Isaac forced a smile and gently tapped Bandy on his beak. Standing up, he picked up another flat stone and skimmed it across the water.

He was about to pick up another rock when he heard a shuffling sound and leaves crunching under someone's or something's feet. He turned quickly and saw two boys standing next to a large poplar tree. They were partially concealed by the foliage. They had been spying on him. The taller boy was lean, with a large oval head and a mop of red hair that curled around the perimeter of his wool cap. The shorter boy was stockier and mean-looking, with a pale round face and bushy black eyebrows. His penetrating brown eyes glared at Isaac. For a few seconds the two boys merely stood there giggling. It was apparent that they were up to no good.

"Well, if it isn't the boy who talks to birds!" the shorter boy taunted, giving his companion a playful punch on the arm. He boldly stepped forward onto the slab of rock facing Isaac, the other boy following him.

"Hello, Barker. I haven't seen yuh at the schoolhouse in a few days. Where yuh been hiding?"

Isaac swallowed nervously. The mean-looking boy was Winfield Scott Mason, son of the president of the First National Bank. The taller boy Isaac only knew as Cooper, but whether that was his given name or surname he did not know. He only knew that where Winfield traveled, Cooper was not far behind.

"What's the little birdie whispering in yer ear today, Barker?" Winfield asked. "Is he telling you about how yer old man is about to default on his mortgage?"

Bandy pecked at Isaac's earlobe. "Don't let him bait you, Isaac!"

Isaac gave his friend a perturbed look. "Quiet, Bandy! He's not baiting me."

The two bullies glanced at one another and burst out laughing at the same time.

"Ha! Ha! Look here, Cooper. Did yuh hear that? He thinks the bloody pigeon spoke to him!"

Isaac's blood began to boil, and he clenched his fists.

"Keehoo! Keehoo! Don't listen to them!" Bandy chirped.

Isaac waved Bandy off and took a step forward. Winfield stood his ground, but Cooper, who lacked the courage of his friend, stepped backward.

"You're a cracked one, Barker," Winfield said. "Talking to birds while yer lazy old man sleeps in his bed all day."

This was more than Isaac was willing to take. He was about the same height as his antagonist, but Winfield was much stockier and the stronger of the two boys.

"Take that back, Winfield, or so help me I'll—"

He never got to finish his sentence. Winfield threw a wild haymaker, but Isaac deftly dodged the blow and, grabbing his opponent's arm, managed to take him off balance. The bigger boy stumbled forward, and Isaac took advantage of this momentary loss of coordination. With a quick push, Winfield landed with a tremendous splash in the cold water. Bandy had taken flight at the first sign of aggression and landed on a branch of a poplar tree where he watched the contest with apprehension.

8

Isaac turned to face Cooper, who had started forward but timidly stopped, noticing Isaac's angry demeanor. The taller boy gave a nervous laugh, showing his buck teeth. He had picked up a stout stick and swung it in front of him, taunting Isaac to try and take it from him. Isaac felt the wind at his back and briefly looked back to see Winfield struggling to swim. The ruffian's large head bobbed up and down in the dark water, his eyes bulging in terror. Isaac felt the blood rush to his head, and he reacted quickly. He turned to Cooper. "Quick! Give me that stick!"

Cooper looked bewildered as Isaac wrestled the stick away from him. He stretched out across the rock on his stomach and held it out for Winfield, who was thrashing about. The bully finally managed to grab hold of it and Isaac pulled him up onto the rock. Winfield sat up. Gasping, he spat out the water that he had inhaled.

"Keehoo! Keehoo!"

Bandy was flying in circles around the boys, and Cooper had a mischievous grin on his long, ugly face. He retrieved the stick that Isaac had just used to fish Winfield out of the water and began swinging it in the air, attempting to connect with the pigeon.

"What's wrong with you? Give me that stick!" Isaac screamed. But when he went to grab hold of it, Cooper swung it down in an arc, striking Isaac on the base of his skull. He heard and felt the sickening *crack* before landing unconscious, face down on the stone slab.

Chapter 2

It was almost dark when Isaac came to his senses. At first, he was completely disoriented, but awareness soon came back to him. He sat up and winced. The throbbing pain in the back of his head told the story. He placed his hand over the spot where the stick had connected and felt a lump. His hand came away sticky with blood. His whole head felt like it was on fire.

"The devil with them," he mumbled. He had saved Winfield's life, and in return they left him out here battered and bruised. He could hear the crickets chirping, and somewhere in the distance a hound was howling—or was it a wolf? For a few minutes he just sat there. Where was Bandy? He was about to call out to him when a soft voice penetrated the lonely darkness.

"Isaac?"

The boy turned his head toward the voice, his eyes adjusting to the darkness. "Bandy! Did they hurt you?"

The pigeon was soon resting on his bloodied friend's shoulder, pecking tenderly at his ear. "I am fine, but you are a mess, Isaac. Please go get patched up. I was so worried you were dead. Please go get patched. Please go get patched."

Isaac struggled to stand up and felt like vomiting. He swayed from side to side before staggering towards the path that led to the road. "I...I'll see you tomorrow, Bandy."

"Oh! Do be careful, Isaac. Do be careful."

Isaac stuffed his hands in his coat and shuffled down the moonlit road. His whole body was stiff, and he felt like his head was about to explode. At one point, he had to stop and find his balance, clinging to the trunk of a beech tree to steady himself. He felt like the whole world was spinning and dropped to his knees and vomited. After that, he felt a little better.

He looked up at the dome of the sky and could see the Seven Sisters. He wondered what time it was. It was late, judging from the position of the stars. The temperature had dropped. He could now see his breath. The night chill caused him to shiver, yet he still had a mile or so to walk before he got home. His mother would be worried. He raised his arms in the air as if he were praying to God and let the icy wind pass through his aching body.

"It is not cold," he mumbled, as if he could deceive himself. He then thought about another problem. He was hungry, despite having just vomited up his last meal. He recalled the meager fare of bread, peas, and onion bulbs that he had passed off as supper to his siblings a few hours earlier. His younger brother, Thomas, had bitterly complained about his small share. Isaac had slapped him out of frustration, causing him to cry. He felt terrible and ended up giving the younger boy half of his own rations. His sisters had just sat there staring at him as if he were the villain.

Suddenly, a thought occurred to him. He would sneak into old Mr. Goodwin's orchard and swipe a few apples for his brother and sisters. No one would ever know. Of course, he risked getting caught by Mr. Goodwin's nephew who lived with him— a fat balding scoundrel appropriately named Killer. At least that is what all the kids called him. Isaac did not know his real name. Anyone daring enough to enter the orchard might feel his wrath. He would take that chance. His stomach growled, angry at him for being neglected.

He stumbled along, listening to the crunching of the leaves under his feet. He was looking for the small path that led into the orchard with its narrow rows of crisp fruit ready to be picked.

Somewhere ahead of him he could hear the screeching of a large feral cat, distant and eerie. He had seen a lynx once. It had casually crossed his path one day on the west side of the pond. It had merely glanced up and ignored him as it sauntered along, but it had frightened him.

The leaves were ankle-deep in the wagon ruts that were also filled with puddles of water from the recent rain. He tried keeping to the shoulder of the road but inevitably found himself stepping in the water. His brogans were soaked, and his feet felt like they were encased in ice.

A noise ahead of him caught his attention and he stopped in his tracks to listen. He was about to dart into the woods when he observed a pale-yellow light reflecting off the trees at the bend of the road. Suddenly, like magic, a carriage appeared, drawn by two healthy stallions. He discerned two figures sitting on the spring seat, one of them holding the reins while the other held a lantern. The driver was a bullish-looking old man. His pockmarked face stood out plainly in the glow of the lantern. The other man was younger. He was a tall, gangly fellow with a wispy blond beard. He recognized the two men immediately as Dr. Benjamin Cutler and his son, Jonas.

"Whoa! Whoa!"

The driver pulled back on the reins and the carriage came to a halt. Isaac stood in the roadway looking lost and cold, staring at the sudden specter that had just materialized out of the night. His gaze

14

focused on the two snorting stallions—their misty exhalations issuing forth from their wet nostrils into the cold night.

"What the devil! Is that you, young Barker?" bellowed Dr. Cutler.

Jonas climbed down, holding the lantern in front of the boy who held his dirty hand up and was squinting at the sudden brightness of the light in his face.

"It's him, Pa!"

The old doctor looked a bit agitated. "Well, don't just stand there. Get up here and have a seat. We have been looking for you for hours!"

Jonas's face was pinched as he held the lantern closer to Isaac's face. "Pa, the boy's been fighting or something. He's a bloody mess!"

"What? Fighting? You don't say," the old doctor said, climbing down to get a better look.

He roughly turned Isaac's head and examined it, using his fingers to probe the wound. There was a two-inch gash at the base of his skull and one of his eyes was slightly swollen. "Jonas, get my bag and a blanket!"

Turning back to Isaac, the doctor led him over to a log and ordered him to sit. Jonas returned quickly with his father's medical bag and the blanket, which he wrapped around the wounded boy's shoulders.

"Hold that lantern closer," the doctor ordered, addressing Jonas. "Fighting, heh? Who roughed you up, boy?"

Isaac's eyes narrowed and he defiantly held up his fist. "There were two of them, Dr. Cutler, and I sent one of them for a drink in the pond but the other hit me with a big stick and knocked me cold! It was Winfield Mason and that Cooper kid. Cooper was the one who thumped me with the stick."

The good doctor smiled as he reached into his medical bag for a bottle of alcohol. "Well, you got spirit, young Barker, that's for sure. Now hold still, this is going to sting."

He dabbed some alcohol on a cloth and held it over the wound. Isaac grimaced but otherwise kept his composure. It would not do for the doctor or Jonas to think him weak. When the doctor had finished wrapping a bandage over his head, he told the boy to climb up onto the buckboard where he sat between the two men. The carriage was soon in motion. This time, with Jonas at the reins. Isaac suddenly realized that they were traveling in a direction away from his house.

"Dr. Cutler, why are we going this way? My home is back there."

He could see the doctor's weary eyes and baggy eyelids above the muffler that he had pulled up to ward off the evening chill. They glanced at him sadly, and it was then Isaac knew something was wrong. Why had they been looking for him? He had spent many nights in the woods, away from home and no one came looking for him. He felt a hollow pit in his stomach.

"You aren't going home, young Barker. There...there has been an accident."

Isaac suddenly felt sick again. "An accident? What...what kind of accident?"

"Well. There was a fire...and...and your mother..." The doctor hesitated, reluctant to tell the boy the horrible news.

"My mother what? What has happened to her?"

"Only your brother survived, Isaac. I...I am sorry."

For a minute or so Isaac was rendered speechless. He felt his whole world crumbling around him. Was it true? Was his mother dead? His sisters? His father? He found it hard to process. He could only sit there staring out at the dark road in front of them.

There had to be some sort of mistake. How could his whole family be dead? It was impossible. He felt himself ushered into some new world where time had just stopped. Reality was gradually setting in. He pulled the wool blanket tighter around his shoulders. His head was no longer throbbing, nor was he hungry. He had forgotten about the apples in Mr. Goodwin's orchard. The carriage rumbled along until it finally stopped in front of a large brick house surrounded by a sturdy wooden fence.

It was then that the magnitude of the situation came to him in a sudden rush of emotion. He buried his head under the blanket, cradled his knees in his arms and let the tears flow in a torrent of anguish.

Chapter 3

The curtains were drawn but a sliver of morning light managed to peek through the window, casting a beam on the small, feathered bed where two boys were sleeping. One of the boys, the younger of the two, sat up and yawned. He swung his feet to the floor and slowly made his way to the window where he parted the curtain and peered out into the yard. He squinted as his eyes adjusted to the light. A tall, elderly man with gray whiskers wearing a stovepipe hat was standing in the driveway. He was talking to Jonas who was standing alongside a richly adorned carriage with fresh green and red paint and velvet curtains. The driver, a middle-aged man, sat on the buckboard looking bored.

For a minute, the boy stood there watching the two men who were engaged in a quiet conversation. Finally, the elderly man followed Jonas into the house. The young boy threw the curtains open so that the whole room was lit. He then ran over and jumped on the bed and began shaking the other boy's shoulders. "Isaac! Isaac! Wake up. There is someone here!"

Isaac turned over. He had an irritated look on his face. "Go back to sleep, Thomas. It's still early."

Thomas was persistent, nudging his brother's shoulder again. "It's light out. Get up! There is a strange man in the house."

Isaac sat up and groaned. It was obvious that he wasn't going to be allowed to sleep. It was Sunday. It had been nearly two weeks since the fire that had killed his parents and two younger sisters. An investigation revealed that the fire had started in the chimney and worked its way up into the loft where everyone but Thomas had been sleeping. The youngster had taken his blanket and curled up next to the fireplace, something he had a habit of doing. By some miracle, he woke up in a cloud of smoke, disoriented and unable to catch his breath. He somehow managed to find his way to the front door and staggered out into the yard where he collapsed. That is where the neighbors found him, but it was too late for the other occupants of the house, who all suffocated in their sleep.

It was still a living nightmare for Isaac, who was buttoning his shirt when he heard a gentle rap on the door. He motioned for Thomas to open it. An old buxom woman stood at the threshold. She was wearing a starched apron. Jane Cutler was younger than her brother, the doctor, but since his wife's death a decade earlier, she had been the woman of the house. A spinster, she was stern and coarse in her mannerisms and the boys feared what she might do if they did not obey her every whim. Isaac was repulsed by the large, hairy brown mole on the tip of her nose. It seemed to twitch every time she spoke, and though it was disgusting to look at, he felt drawn toward it as if it were a target.

"Get dressed and meet us in the parlor," she said roughly. "There is someone here to see you."

"Yes, ma'am," the boys responded.

After she shut the door, Isaac finished dressing and helped his brother with his shoes.

"Who do you think it is?" Thomas asked, watching Isaac lace his shoe.

The older boy shrugged. "I don't know. Perhaps it is our uncle."

Isaac had thought about this possibility. He had only met his great-uncle Raymond once. He remembered him as a stern, arrogant man who lived in the elite Back Bay of Boston. He had made his wealth in the shipping industry. Raymond Barker was a widower with no children of his own. It would only stand to reason that he would be interested in adopting his late nephew's children. As far as Isaac knew, he was their only living relative.

Isaac adjusted the collar on his brother's coat and gave him a look-over before brushing the younger boy's brown curls with his ivory handle comb.

"Chin up, Thomas. Come now. They are waiting for us."

Thomas's eyes were big. A worried look was on his face, but he trusted his big brother. In fact, he revered him as an almost God-like figure.

The two boys entered the parlor. They found Dr. Cutler and the strange man in conversation, seated in two leather chairs in front of the blazing hearth. It was the strange man who first perceived their entrance. He had removed his stovepipe hat, revealing a bald head and bushy gray eyebrows. His eyes narrowed as he beckoned for the timid youths to approach.

"You don't remember me, do you?" the old man said with a gruff voice.

Isaac nodded. "I remember you, Uncle. Father took me to Boston when I was nine. We visited your house on the bay."

Raymond Barker gripped the armrests of his chair and pushed himself forward. He studied the boys as if they were merchandise on the quay, waiting to be loaded onto one of his ships. Isaac could not help but notice his cane. It was an expensive ivory one, with a silver eagle on the top.

"I remember. Your father came to beg me for money," Raymond said.

Isaac's face reddened. "My father never would have done that, sir."

The old man gripped the handle of his cane and firmly pounded the floor with it. Thomas clutched his brother's arm nervously. "Are you calling me a liar, sonny?"

"No, sir. I just remember it differently, that's all, sir," Isaac responded.

Raymond Barker was chewing on his bottom lip. He was about to respond to his nephew when they were interrupted by Jane, who entered the parlor with a silver tray. She set it down on the small oak table in between the two men and poured them each a cup of tea. Her gaze met her brother's, who seemed to be a bit disturbed by their visitor's outburst.

"There is sugar and cream on the tray if you desire it," Jane said, directing her comment at Raymond but not waiting for a response. She left the room, and the old man turned his attention back to his older nephew.

"You are an impertinent child. I should hold the belt to you, but you look so sickly that I might break you in two pieces!"

Isaac swallowed nervously. He could feel his brother's hand tighten on his arm. Raymond reached around and grabbed the younger boy's wrist and pulled him forward.

"And what is your name, you timid soul? I have forgotten it. I don't believe we have ever met."

"T-Thomas, sir," the boy said, his eyes filling with tears.

"How old are you?"

"I'm seven, sir," Thomas replied, meekly.

The old man let go of his wrist and turned his attention to the tea, adding a sugar cube and stirring it with a small silver spoon. His gray whiskers twitched as he tasted it. Ignoring the boys, he directed his conversation to the good doctor who was sitting with his legs crossed, sipping his tea.

"Dr. Cutler, I'll be taking these boys with me. I have no heirs and they shall assist an old man in the twilight of his life. The younger one shall attend school as will the older one. First, though, I have a job for the older one. We will see if he has mettle."

The doctor seemed interested and carried on the conversation as if the boys were not even in the room. "Well, I can tell you, Mr. Barker, the older one is a bright boy, but prone to fighting. I do think you should take great care to treat the boys somewhat tenderly. They have both been through a rough spot the last few weeks, and I cannot help but pity their condition."

Raymond cleared his throat, his eyes once again falling on the two boys, who merely stood there in front of him, feeling awkward and unsure of what to do.

"I will take a different approach, Dr. Cutler. They should know that this world in which they live is not fit for weaklings. They need to become hardened to the conditions, and if they cannot adapt, they shall be swallowed by the vipers that prey on them. No, sir, they shall get no coddling from me. But I will be fair and fatherly."

The doctor set his tea down on the table and glanced at the two youths. "Well, there is no more to be said about it. Isaac, Thomas, go pack your things."

Isaac took his brother's hand and left the room, leaving the two men to finish their conversation. The boys quickly packed their meager belongings into two seabags the doctor had given them. The fire had left them nothing from their old life. Miss Cutler had taken them down to the clothing store. She fitted them each with two sets of pantaloons and shirts, along with socks and new shoes for which the boys were grateful. Jonas, too, had contributed to their dire condition. He had given Thomas a dozen tin soldiers and bought a new wool cap for Isaac.

When the boys were finished packing, they returned to the parlor where they found Jonas adding logs to the fire. He turned and waved at them before resuming his task. They walked out into the morning sunshine with their seabags slung over their shoulders. They found the doctor in an animated conversation with their new guardian, who had already climbed up into the carriage.

"Come now! Make haste! It doesn't do to dawdle!" the uncle yelled at the boys.

The boys threw their bags into the carriage. Isaac turned to the doctor and held out his hand. He was reluctant to leave the good doctor and venture into this new beginning with a stern uncle he barely knew. "Thank you, sir. You were most kind to me and my brother. I shall not forget it."

Dr. Cutler took the boy's hand and smiled. "If you ever need anything, young Isaac, I shall be here."

The carriage rumbled away leaving a cloud of dust behind it. Isaac looked back and could see Jonas standing in the doorway, watching them leave. Finally, they turned around a bend in the road and the house disappeared from their view.

Isaac was sitting next to his brother on one of the two plush bench seats, while their uncle sat across from them, smoking his ivory pipe. Isaac was ruminating on the sudden turn of events when he thought about Bandy. It dawned on him that he had not gone back to visit him as he had promised. He had been too busy.

As the carriage moved along the dusty highway, he realized that they would be passing by Bandy's pond and decided he must try to contact his feathered friend.

As they neared the place, he parted the silk curtain and stuck his head out the window, letting the cool breeze blow his flaxen locks across his face. He began to whistle loudly, a singular piping sound that Bandy would recognize. He glanced over at his uncle who had lowered his pipe, his face twisted in confusion.

"Boy, what manner of tomfoolery is this?"

Isaac smiled. "I am calling a friend, Uncle Raymond."

The old man studied the boy, his gray eyebrows coming together to form a single line. He shook his head and closed his eyes. When he opened them again, he seemed shocked at what he saw. A passenger pigeon had flown through the open window and alighted on Isaac's shoulder. Isaac rubbed its belly and whispered something to it.

"Keehoo! Keehoo!"

The bird flapped its wings and disappeared back into the sunny morning sky. Isaac shot a glance at his uncle who was once again puffing on his pipe, blowing circles of smoke into the air.

"Boy, you seem to have a knack for pigeons. Where did you learn that?"

Isaac shrugged. "I...I don't really know, sir. I suppose it comes natural to me."

"Hmm. Well, they were not wrong when they told me you were a bright one."

The carriage continued onto the Boston Post Road. After a quick lunch of apples and biscuits, the rest of the journey was quiet except for when a carriage wheel struck a rut in the road. This would jostle the three passengers around and cause a flurry of curses from the irritable old man, directed at the driver.

It was almost dark when they reached Boston. Isaac peered out at the crowded streets lined with vendors of all kinds. He recognized the old North Church and remembered his father telling him about Paul Revere.

A slattern dressed in rags accosted the carriage, begging for money when they were forced to stop for traffic on the roadway. The old woman was toothless, with pinched cheeks and bloodshot eyes. She reminded Isaac of the old hag, Jenny Greenteeth. His mother had tried to scare him from going to Bandy's pond when he was young. She would tell him that old, wicked Jenny would rise out of the pond's murky depths and pull him under the water. However, he did not get frightened easily and this tall tale did little to prevent his ventures to that hallowed place.

"Have ye a penny for a poor wretch?" the old woman asked, sticking her haggard head into the carriage.

Thomas edged closer to his brother. The grotesque appearance of the woman frightened him.

"Here, take this and go, woman!" Uncle Raymond said, reaching into his purse and handing her a penny. "There are charitable houses for people like you!"

She gave him a wicked look and disappeared back into the crowded street. Isaac watched her accost another well-to-do Boston blueblood, but this man sent her scampering away with his cane. The boy turned to his uncle who had once again lit his pipe.

"Why did you give her a penny, Uncle Raymond?"

"You ask too many questions, boy," he responded, blowing rings with his pipe. "Let's just say that I believe in a little Christian charity," he added.

Eventually, the carriage started rolling again. It was dark when they finally pulled up to the large iron gate in front of the Barker mansion. The full moon was high in the sky, throwing its beams of light down on them. Thomas had fallen asleep, his head resting on his brother's shoulder. Isaac gazed out at the bay, the moonlight shimmering off the water. To him, the last few weeks had been surreal, almost as if he had been dreaming and had yet to awaken. He nudged his brother, who sat up, yawning, and rubbing his tired eyes.

Isaac peered out into the darkness and looked up at the foreboding iron gate guarded by two stone lions. They seemed to be glaring at him. A bald man wearing dark tails appeared at the gate like a phantom, unlocking it and motioning for the carriage to proceed into the yard. It pulled up in front of the house and once again the bald man appeared, this time opening the carriage door and assisting Uncle Raymond down. Isaac and Thomas grabbed their duffel bags and started to follow their uncle, but the bald man stopped them. In the moonlight, Isaac noticed a hideous scar that ran down his left cheek from his eye, almost to the corner of his mouth.

"Master Barker, ah'll take that," he said with an accent, pointing to the duffel bag slung over Isaac's shoulder. He had already dispossessed Thomas of his bag. The younger boy seemed transfixed by the size of the house, his eyes wide with anticipation of what it was like inside.

"I can handle it, sir," Isaac replied.

"Master, I insist."

The bald man seemed irritated, and Isaac thought it best to pass it off to him. The two boys followed him into the large foyer. A magnificent brass chandelier with silver candlesticks hung from the ceiling, lighting up the room. Thomas pulled on his brother's arm and pointed to a medieval suit of armor near the entrance.

Their uncle had disappeared into an adjoining room without saying another word to them. They followed the bald man into the hallway and passed a small library. Isaac caught a glimpse of a young woman of African heritage sitting in a leather chair, reading a book by candlelight. For a moment, their eyes met as she looked up from her book.

The bald man led them up a marble staircase to the second level. Although Isaac had been here before, this was the first time he had ever been inside the mansion. It was overwhelming. He had never seen such wealth in his short life, and he wondered if he was dreaming. They were led down a long, carpeted hallway and into a small room. The bald man set their two bags down on a chest and ambled over to the window to close the shutters. The room was drafty, but there were two comfortable feathered beds and wool blankets.

"There is a pitcher of water on the nightstand and the water closet is across the hall if y'all should need it. If yuh require my assistance, yuh need only ring the bell near the door. By the way, Ah'm yuh manservant, Charles. Good night."

He turned and started to leave, but Isaac called him back. "Will Uncle come to see us?"

Charles was rubbing his square chin, his gray eyebrows twitching slightly. "He is busy, Master Isaac. Y'all will see him in the morning."

Without saying another word, Charles shut the door, leaving the two boys alone in the darkness, the only light coming from a thick candle hanging in a sconce on the wall.

"What's a manservant, Isaac?" Thomas asked.

Isaac shrugged, pulling the blanket over him. "I guess he waits on us...like a butler, I suppose."

Thomas was still sitting up, looking fearfully at the candle flame flickering in the darkness. He grabbed his blanket and made his way over to his brother's bed.

"Isaac, can I sleep with you? I don't like this place. It's too big."

The older boy poked his head out from under his blanket. He frowned but reluctantly motioned for his brother to lay down beside him. "Okay, but don't be kicking and rolling about."

Thomas smiled. He jumped into the bed and wrapped himself in his blanket. For a few minutes neither boy spoke, each wrapped up in his own thoughts. Finally, Thomas broke the silence. "Isaac, why did Momma and Papa have to die? I miss them."

Isaac turned his head. He could see the profile of his brother's head in the candlelight. Despite now being under their uncle's care, he still felt responsible for Thomas. "I don't know, Thomas. I miss them, too."

Thomas held up one of his hands and could see its elongated shadow on the wall. He moved his fingers, creating the illusion of a quacking duck. "Isaac, you...you aren't going to die, are you?"

The older boy swallowed and tried closing his eyes. "No, Thomas. I'm not going to die. Now go to sleep, okay?"

"Okay, Isaac."

The younger boy was soon asleep, but Isaac had too much on his mind. His uncle had told him he had a job for him to do. What kind of job? he wondered, his mind racing. He had asked his uncle about it in the carriage, but the old man brushed his inquiries aside and only told him he would learn about it in the morning.

Would he be sent away? Only a few weeks earlier he had been dirt poor. Now here he was, with his own personal manservant. It was all so incredibly unbelievable. Did his uncle really care about them? He was a stern old widower with a rough exterior but there was also a glimmer of goodness in him. After all, he had given that old hag a penny. He couldn't be all that bad.

And who was that young woman sitting in the library? He had only seen her for a second but for some reason he felt she exuded an aura of sadness. Then there was Bandy. He had followed the carriage and was somewhere, perhaps perched on the branch of a tree looking out at the bay.

For the longest time he listened to his brother's light snores and thought about the future. Finally, mercifully, he drifted off to sleep.

Chapter 4

Morning came quickly. A soft tap on the door was followed by light footsteps traveling across the creaking boards of the bedroom floor. The shutters were flung open revealing another sunny morning. Isaac squinted into the rays of sunshine that flooded the room. He sat up, stretched, and glanced over at the lump covered in blankets next to him. He nudged his brother. "Get up, Thomas."

Charles placed two towels on the washstand and filled the basin with water from the pitcher. He then pointed to a large wooden closet next to it. "Y'all will find a change of clothes suitable for your new station in there. Y'all are to meet your uncle in the dinin' room in half an hour to break your fast. Do not be late."

Isaac nodded and watched the strange man leave the room. There was something odd about the manservant, but he could not quite place what it was. He had a strange accent, but so did a lot of other people he had met. For some inexplicable reason, he did not trust him, but he did not know why.

After washing, he pulled open the wardrobe, revealing an array of rich clothing. There were dress jackets and pressed cotton pants of

36

various sizes, along with expensive leather shoes with brass buttons and laces. White and gray billowy shirts with cuff links hung on hangers. Uncle Raymond had obviously prepared for their arrival.

Isaac picked out a suit for himself and one that would fit his brother. They were soon washed and dressed. Thomas stood in front of the large mirror on the wall, wearing a dull frown.

"Isaac, these clothes are stiff. Why can't I wear my old ones?" Thomas complained.

"Because I said so, and it is Uncle's wish. Do not be ungrateful. Now come along."

Isaac had chosen one of the billowy white shirts and a pressed jacket and tie. When he stood in front of the mirror, he couldn't help but think of what his nemesis Winfield would think of him now. He looked quite the dandy. The shoes were a little big, but he figured he would grow into them. After all, he was only thirteen and still had a lot of growing to do. Thomas began complaining about his shoes being too tight, but Isaac hurried him along and told him to be polite.

Charles was waiting for them in the hall. He led them back down the marble staircase and into the dining room. Isaac was surprised to see the young lady he had seen in the library the night before already seated at the table.

She appeared to be about eighteen years old. She wore long braids that encompassed a small oval face. She watched them come in and smiled. The boys sat across from her.

An older woman appeared from the kitchen. She was carrying a tray of tea and crumpets and set it down on the table. She then poured the tea into cups for the boys and the young lady but did not fill the fourth cup at the head of the table. Isaac presumed this would be where his uncle sat. Thomas nudged his brother and, leaning close to him, pointed to the young woman who was watching them with what appeared to be wry amusement.

"Who is she?" Thomas whispered in his brother's ear.

The older boy shrugged and was about to chastise his brother for being rude when the girl finally spoke. "I am Esther. You must be Isaac and Thomas."

Thomas nodded, an exaggerated movement of his head which elicited a slight chuckle from the girl.

"I am Isaac, and this is Thomas," the older boy replied, placing a hand on his brother's shoulder. "I saw you in the library last night when we were coming in."

The girl wet her lips and took a sip of tea. "I know. I saw you, too. Father told me you were coming."

"Father?" Isaac asked. "Who is your father?"

The girl laughed, showing her gleaming white teeth. "Your uncle. He didn't tell you?"

Isaac shook his head. He looked at his brother who appeared just as bewildered.

"He didn't tell me he had a daughter," Isaac responded. "But I...I don't understand...How?"

This response caused Esther to laugh even harder. "You mean, how can I, being Black, be a daughter to your very white uncle?"

Isaac nodded. He felt stupid but when he realized that her merriment was directed at his brother and not him, he found the laughter contagious. Thomas's mouth was open, his eyes wide with disbelief. He was pointing at Esther but looking at Isaac for answers.

"Let me explain," Esther said, but she was interrupted by a bell ringing and the double doors opening from the adjoining kitchen. This was followed by a booming voice and the appearance of Raymond Barker.

"And tell him not to overcook the eggs, damn it! Unless he wants them dumped over his head!"

He shuffled over to his chair and took a seat at the head of the table, glancing first at Esther and then at the two boys who sat erect in their chairs watching him nervously.

"Damn idiot never gets it right. The only reason I keep him on is because he can dish up a wonderful London broil! Otherwise, out he would go! Out in the street! Out in the cold!"

Esther was wearing a smirk.

Uncle Raymond unfolded his napkin and tucked it into his collar. He then picked up his teacup and began banging on it with his spoon. "Mary? Where are you, woman? What does it take to be served a cup of tea these days?"

The old woman appeared from the kitchen in a flash, steam issuing from the kettle. She performed the delicate task of filling the old man's cup as he watched her shaking hand.

"I'm sorry, Mr. Barker. I was helping Emilio with the eggs," she said apologetically.

"Thank you, Mary. There is no need to help Emilio. You know how I like to chide him. It is in jest. He gives it right back to me! The damn Portuguese rascal! I'll throw him out in the cold one of these days!"

He took a sip of his tea and made eye contact with Esther who had folded her arms across her chest and was mildly shaking her head.

"What is it, Esther? What have I done now, my dear girl?"

"You didn't tell the boys you had a daughter. Why not?"

Uncle Raymond rolled his tired gray eyes and tugged on his pointed beard. "I plum forgot! Don't chastise me, dear. I can assure you it was quite unintentional. I did have other things on my mind, you know."

Esther shrugged. "I was getting ready to tell the boys about how I came to be your daughter. They seemed mystified. I shall tell them... unless you prefer to do it yourself?"

"No, you go right ahead," he said, taking a sip of his tea.

She turned back to the two boys who sat there patiently, still unable to comprehend the drastic change in their lives.

"Well, I was born a slave eighteen summers ago in Virginia. I never knew my father. He was sold to a farmer shortly after I was born. I only know his name was Ox."

"Ox! That's a funny name!" Thomas said with a giggle.

"My mother said they called him Ox because he was as strong as an ox. My mother died when I was ten and left me with my half-sister, Joy, who is now about your age, Isaac."

Isaac seemed puzzled. "Is Joy here, too?"

"No. I will get to that, but first let me tell you about my former master. He was a wicked man named, Wil Jericho. He runs a plantation just outside of Suffolk, Virginia. His wife, though, is a kind woman. For the life of me I do not know why she married that beast of a man, but life is full of mysteries, you know. She took a liking to me and Joy. We worked as house domestics and every day before we went to work, she would sit us down and teach us writing and mathematics. I have managed to learn a lot, but my sister, Joy, makes me look dumb. Mrs. Jericho taught her elementary mathematics, but she soon surpassed her teacher's skill. Mrs. Jericho bought her books on geometry and physics, and she devoured them. Of course, this was all dangerous ground we were treading."

"What was so dangerous about it?" asked Isaac.

"It is illegal in Virginia to teach a slave to read and write, never mind mathematics. When Wil Jericho found out, he was livid. He beat me and Joy, and sold me to your uncle who was visiting the plantation at the time. He purchased my freedom and took me with him back here to Massachusetts. You see, your uncle is what they call an abolitionist."

Isaac had heard of the term. He knew that an abolitionist was someone who was against slavery, but he had to confess he knew little else about that wicked institution.

"But what about Joy? Is she still a slave?" Isaac asked.

Esther nodded. "Unfortunately, yes. Father tried to purchase her freedom also, but Wil Jericho is a vindictive man. He refused. It has been two years since I left Virginia but now something has changed. I will let Father tell you what it is, but first it appears our breakfast is ready."

Mary set down a platter of fried eggs and toast, serving Esther first and then Uncle Raymond. She left Thomas for last and when the boy went to dig into his fare, his brother tapped him on the wrist, stopping him.

"Mind your manners, Thomas. We say grace, first," he whispered, hoping his uncle did not notice. But nothing got by the old man. However, instead of chastising the young boy, he merely nodded his approval at Isaac's reprimand.

Esther said grace and they began eating. Isaac wanted desperately to know what job his uncle had planned for him but was reluctant to bring up the subject while they were eating. When they were done breaking their fast, Uncle Raymond clapped his hands.

"Which brings us to the job that I have for you, Isaac."

Isaac swallowed the last piece of his toast and put down his fork. He was all ears.

Uncle Raymond continued, "Esther told you something has changed regarding her sister. A few weeks ago, I received a telegram from Wil Jericho. He is willing to let me buy Joy's freedom, but unfortunately my deteriorating health will prevent me from traveling to Virginia to complete the transaction. I would never survive the journey, my dear boy. You, however, young, energetic, and smart, will act as my agent. I have wired the sum he has requested, but you will need to sign the bill of sale on my behalf in front of a notary in Virginia. They require it. Joy can then be given her papers. She will be a free girl! You, young man, have been delegated with an important task."

Isaac was speechless. He glanced around the room. Esther seemed to be watching his face for any sign of emotion, but she was to be disappointed. He merely cleared his throat and looked down at the few crumbs of food left on his plate.

"I...I'm going to Virginia?"

"You leave next Friday, if you choose," his uncle said, placing his fork down and folding his old arthritic hands in front of him.

"By myself?"

"No, Charles, your manservant, will be going with you. There is something else. Esther, you tell the boy what it is, my dear."

The young girl nodded. "Wil Jericho is not doing this out of the goodness of his heart. Joy suffers from terrible headaches. The doctor in Virginia believes she might have a tumor, but without operating, they do not know for sure.

We…we do not know the severity of it, but apparently it is sufficient cause for Wil Jericho to make some money. There…there is a doctor here in Boston that gives us hope. If she can make the journey with your assistance…well…then…"

Esther's eyes became moist, and Isaac saw a tear roll down her cheek before she lowered her head.

"Now, now, my dear. It will be all right," Uncle Raymond said. "If young Isaac here agrees to go, Joy will be with us in no time. No time at all."

She looked up and directed her gaze at Isaac, who swallowed hard and was chewing nervously on his lower lip. He turned to his uncle. "You mean…I…I have a choice? To go or not to go?"

"Of course, you do, lad. Life is full of choices. Now, finish your tea. You do not have to give us your decision at this very moment."

Isaac looked over at Esther. He had taken a liking to her and knew what he had to do. He stood up.

"No, sir. I will give you my decision right now. You are wrong. I do not have a choice. Esther's sister needs me. I will go, sir, and I will bring Joy back with me."

He watched Esther's expression go from one of sorrow to sheer joy. Unable to restrain her emotions, she stood up and within a few seconds was embracing the boy as if she had known him forever.

"Thank you! Oh, thank you, Isaac!"

"Can I go, too?" Thomas asked. This caused all present to turn their attention to the younger boy. He only knew that his brother was going far away, and he wanted to be with him. Isaac sat down and placed a hand on his brother's shoulder.

"Thomas, I promise I will be back. I must do this. You will be here with Esther and Uncle Raymond. They will take good care of you. Do you understand?"

Thomas nodded, but his face betrayed the sadness overwhelming him, and he began to cry, hugging his big brother.

"But...but I want to go with you, Isaac," Thomas said, rubbing his red eyes.

Uncle Raymond cleared his throat. He had lit his pipe and soon the whole room smelled like a smoking room. "Esther, take young Thomas outside and show him the fountain. I need to talk to Isaac in private, please."

"Yes, Father, of course."

The girl took Thomas by the hand and led him out into the hallway. Esther closed the door and left the uncle alone with his nephew for the first time.

"You made the right decision, Isaac. I commend you for it."

The boy nodded. "It was an easy choice, Uncle. Though I do hate it for Thomas. I am all he has left. I do wish he could come with me, but it wouldn't do, would it?"

The old man was gazing at the far wall, seemingly in deep thought, his pipe hanging from his lips, supported by his thumb and forefinger. Isaac was not sure what to make of his uncle. He was an enigma, that much was certain to him.

"Well," Raymond said, tapping on his pipe. "I will give you the necessary documents to act on my behalf. You do know this is unprecedented. You are still a minor, but I have convinced a state judge in Virginia to let you be my agent. We are a blood relation, you know. Of course, when I pass from this realm to my heavenly reward, you shall inherit my wealth with the stipulation that you provide for your brother and my adopted daughter. My attorney—Robert Metcalf is his name—will guide you through the conundrum of my vast holdings. You can trust him."

Isaac felt as if he were living in a dream, an alternate reality. He found it all quite overwhelming. His whole life had changed in the blink of an eye. He closed his eyes and breathed in the smoke from his uncle's pipe.

For almost an hour they sat there chatting about the shipping business, and Isaac was surprised to discover he actually had a good understanding of it. His uncle took him into the library and showed him books on economics, including Adam Smith's *Wealth of Nations* and books by David Ricardo and John Stuart Mill. He had heard of these books but never read them. Uncle Raymond then reached up and pulled down a volume from the top shelf. It was an old book, and he blew the dust off it. He handed it to Isaac who peered at it wonderingly.

"It is a slave narrative," the old man said, tapping the bowl of his pipe. "Have you ever heard of Gustavus Vassa?"

Isaac shook his head as he leafed through the yellowed pages.

"Take it and read it. It will give you a better understanding of the evil institution of slavery. I will leave you now. Feel free to walk the grounds and explore the house. It is your home now."

Uncle Raymond started to leave the library, but as he reached the doorway he turned back to Isaac. "One more thing, Isaac. I apologize for the way I treated you when we first met. I am old and sometimes ornery. At times I do not think about other people's feelings. I misspoke. Your father did not beg me for money. He asked for a loan, and I gave it to him. He would not take charity."

Isaac watched him leave with mixed feelings. He decided to take a walk. He would find Bandy and tell him the news. Setting the book down on a chair, he walked out into the cool morning.

There was a cold breeze coming off the bay and he stuffed his hands into the pockets of his suit jacket. He felt stiff and suddenly longed for his old, comfortable clothes. He gazed around him at his new surroundings and caught a glimpse of Esther and Thomas walking along the beach. A clipper ship sat in the bay, at anchor, its sails furled. He wondered if it was one of his uncle's ships. He headed for the orchard behind the servants' quarters and plucked an apple from one of the trees, a big fat red one that tasted sweet. He suddenly realized he no longer had to worry about stealing apples. There were plenty of them here, and who was going to chastise him for picking a few?

He had always thought of stealing as distasteful. He never would have done so for himself but found it hard to watch his younger siblings suffer.

He was just finishing his first apple when he heard the familiar call of his feathered friend.

"Keehoo! Keehoo!"

Bandy was perched on the sturdy limb of an apple tree. When Isaac spotted him, his face brightened.

"Bandy!"

The pigeon flew from the branch and landed on Isaac's shoulder, tenderly pecking him on his ear. "Isaac, Isaac. I have missed you. What is the meaning of this? The carriage ride here to this distant place?"

Isaac mumbled something and sat down on a rock. Bandy flapped his wings and swapped shoulders.

"I'm going away, Bandy. Far away—to Virginia. I must bring a girl back. I am a sort of escort for her, but I'll be back...I'll be back and when I am, we can go back to the pond and visit with all our friends! We can have a big reunion. You can invite Tom Turkey and Mother Deer and her little fawns. We can have a grand time on the rock!"

Bandy became excited and began flying around his friend. The wind was blowing Isaac's flaxen hair across his face, which was beaming with anticipation for the event that was still weeks, possibly months, away.

For the next hour, Isaac played games with Bandy—hide-and-seek was their favorite. He used the orchard to full advantage. Finally, Isaac realized he would have to take his leave from his feathered friend. It was time to say goodbye. He thought about Thomas. He must be missing him by now, and Esther, too, would wonder where he had been off to.

"Keehoo! Keehoo!"

Bandy gave Isaac a friendly peck on his red cheek. The boy watched him fly up over the trees and become a speck before finally disappearing into the light of the autumn sun. Isaac felt a tear roll down his cheek as he slowly made his way back toward the mansion.

Chapter 5

saac and Charles boarded the packet steamship, *Pegasus,* at the Norwich docks where the captain himself showed them a first-class cabin, complete with two bunks, a washbasin, and towels.

They had taken the train from Boston. Isaac had felt a lump in his throat as he watched Thomas waving at him from the station platform with Esther and Byron, Uncle Raymond's driver, at his side. That had been early this morning, before dawn. It was now late afternoon, and it would be dark soon.

Isaac took a stroll out onto the deck and watched as the steamship was released from its mooring masts and headed out into the river. Clouds of thick black smoke belched above the two tall smokestacks as the firemen shoveled coal into the furnace. The *Pegasus* gathered steam and its gigantic paddle wheels went to work, pushing the vessel farther out into the river, quickly leaving the quay behind them. A few seagulls followed in its wake, hoping to snag a crumb from the bevy of people standing along the deck.

Isaac could see the lights from the city glowing like coals from a dying fire. He pulled his cloak tightly around his neck to ward off the evening chill. He wondered what Thomas was doing. Although his brother could be a pest, he loved him and felt responsible for his well-being. He would do his duty, perform his business, and return. Thomas would be fine in the care of Esther and Uncle Raymond.

He was just about to return to his cabin when he detected the presence of someone standing beside him. The man was well-dressed, wearing long gray tails and a soft wool cap. He appeared to be in his mid-thirties but could have been older. The man's whiskers and thick droopy black moustache were speckled with gray. He stuck his hand out.

"Major Samuel Frost, at your service. And you are?"

Isaac looked at the man's extended gloved hand and shook it. "Isaac Barker, sir."

"And where do you hail from, young Isaac Barker? I could not help noticing that you occupy the other first-class cabin. Who is the odd-looking gentleman with the Virginia accent who travels with you? Not your father, I presume. He was rather rude to me on the quay."

"No, sir, he is my servant. My uncle is Raymond Barker, a merchant out of Boston. I travel on business on his behalf to Suffolk, Virginia."

The major looked surprised. He cocked an eyebrow, and Isaac watched him tapping his gloved fingers along the rail as if he were playing a piano.

"Business? Virginia? For your uncle? If I am being too nosy, you need only tell me to mind my business," the major said, folding his arms across his chest.

"No, sir, I don't mind me telling you, sir," Isaac replied. He related the details of his mission and noticed the major's countenance change from one of curious introspection to one of concern.

"There is danger where you go, young Isaac. Have you not heard the news?"

Isaac shook his head. "No, sir."

"Lincoln has been elected president. It is official. It came over the wire only minutes before we left Norwich."

This news had no effect on Isaac. He had heard of Abraham Lincoln, but why should his elevation to the presidency jeopardize his traveling to Virginia?

"I don't understand," Isaac said.

Major Frost explained. "The southern states are worried that a Lincoln presidency will usher in a wave of new laws, regulating slavery and states rights. There are talks of secession and possible rebellion."

The boy frowned. "Well, I'll finish my uncle's business and be back in Massachusetts in a few days."

Isaac was just about ready to turn in when he spied a mother and a young girl of about six years of age sitting against the bulwark, shivering under a thin blanket. He turned to say something to the major. However, the good man had lit his pipe and drifted away from him, seemingly preoccupied with watching a passing steamer in the distance. The *Pegasus* had steamed out past New London into Block Island Sound. Its first port of call was Jersey City, where it would let off passengers and restock the coal and wood bins. From there, they would steam to Norfolk, where Isaac would hire a coach to Jericho Plantation.

Isaac walked over to where the two bedraggled passengers sat huddled together. They must have booked passage in steerage, which meant they would have to manage the night in the crowded area below deck or out here under the stars.

He removed his cloak and wrapped it around the little girl whose big brown eyes were glued to him. The mother said something to him in a foreign tongue that he did not understand. He thought that it might be Italian, but it could just as well have been French.

He motioned for them to follow him. He opened his cabin door to find Charles sitting on the bottom bunk looking over some papers by candlelight. The servant quickly pushed them under his blanket, which raised the suspicions of Isaac. He wondered if his uncle's faith in the man was misplaced.

"Who are these beggars?" Charles demanded.

Isaac merely glanced at his traveling companion, who was now holding his hands over the grated vent in the floor, from which heat from the steam below, issued forth, making the cabin nice and warm. His disagreeable profile looked sinister in the candlelight.

"They are cold and in need of succor," Isaac responded. "I cannot in good conscience leave this young girl shivering away the cold night while I lay warm in my bunk."

Charles looked disgusted.

"They are Dagos, just off the boat. Not fit for the company of the likes of you and me," he said. "Now send them back out!"

Isaac felt a rage boiling up inside him. Who was this man to talk to him like this? He started to bite his tongue, gathering the courage to speak plainly. Wasn't this man his servant? Well, by God, if he was, he would have to be put in his place.

"I'll not send them out into the cold. And how dare you talk to me like that? Mind your place, sir!" Isaac exclaimed with authority.

Isaac could not believe what he had just said. Charles stood up, furious. Isaac shivered slightly with fear. The servant was a big man and could easily hurt him if he had a mind to. For a few seconds, he glared at the boy, his chiseled face radiating the hate within him. Then, suddenly, his face softened, and he sat back on his bunk.

"Well, I'll not give up my bunk for them. If you want to give them yours, so be it."

Isaac relaxed, the crisis at an end. He could hardly believe it. He had shown his hand and won. He looked at the two immigrants who sat wide-eyed in a corner of the cabin, and he motioned for them to climb onto the top bunk, which they did with many thanks in the Italian tongue. Isaac retrieved his cloak and stepped back out into the cold night.

Charles was behind him in the doorway. "Where are you going, Master Isaac?"

"I'll make do out here. There is no place to stretch out on the floor because of the basin," the boy responded. "Go to your bunk and leave me be, but molest the woman or girl and I shall have you turned into the drink. Do you understand?"

Charles's lips were pursed. He had a look on his face as though he wanted nothing more than to throttle this lowborn boy who had suddenly found himself thrust into a position of prominence.

"I will not turn them out, Master Isaac. Have a splendid night shivering out in the cold."

Charles shut the door, and Isaac heard the bolt slam home. He sat down against the bulwark, pulling his warm cloak around him to ward off the cold. A few other people were up on the deck, unable to find places to lay their weary heads in the crowded common space below. He buried his head between his knees and closed his eyes. They were not closed long when he felt someone nudging his shoulder. He looked up to see the tall form of Major Frost, his gloved hand extended.

"Come on, lad. I heard it all. I have an extra bunk, but I have a right mind to teach that bully servant of yours a lesson."

Isaac took his new friend's hand, and he was pulled to his feet. They were soon sitting on the major's bunk, sipping mugs of hot chocolate that the good man had ordered from the scullery. The major was eyeing the boy with admiration.

"Well, lad, chivalry is not dead. You proved that tonight," he said, placing a hand on the boy's shoulder. "If one day I have a son, I hope he is like you."

Isaac shrugged. "Well, I only did what I thought was right, sir."

"An admirable gesture. Lacking these days. Now, tell me about this servant of yours. He is a rogue, naturally. Your uncle trusts him?"

"Yes, sir, I think so. But I do not like him. He acts strange. I...I saw him shuffling some papers around in the cabin when I walked in on him just now. I think he is hiding something from Uncle and me."

The major took a sip of his chocolate. He then placed his mug down on the floor, opened his small chest, and retrieved a quill and some ink, along with a piece of paper. He hastily wrote down two addresses and handed the paper to Isaac, who looked at it curiously.

"Young Isaac, my destination is Fort Norfolk. I am an ordnance officer, and the army has decided to reinforce the garrison there. I suspect there will be trouble with all this secessionist talk going around, and that is why they are taking these precautionary steps. If you need any help, do not hesitate to call on me, son."

Isaac studied the handwriting and noted that the second address was not a place in Norfolk. His friend noticed the confusion cross his face.

"You mentioned you will be escorting a young lady, a slave. That second address is a safehouse. If you need a place of refuge, you will find succor there," the major said quietly.

Isaac folded the paper and stuffed it safely in his cloak. He took a sip of his chocolate, feeling its hospitable warmth.

"Major Frost, I thank you, sir. I hope to be done with this business in a few days and back in Massachusetts."

The good man nodded. He finished the last of his chocolate and waited for the boy to finish his. "Well, son, it is late, and this crate will be boisterous in a few hours when we reach Jersey City. Let's get a little sleep while we can."

Isaac climbed up on the top bunk and watched the major blow out the candle, leaving them in the darkness. It wasn't long before he could hear the major's snores above the din of the steamship's engine.

He, however, was wide awake. He suddenly felt homesick. He wanted nothing more than to be back home at his sacred place at Bandy's pond, talking to his animal friends. What was he doing here? It would have been unfathomable only a few weeks earlier.

As he sat on his bunk musing, a sudden thought occurred to him. Major Frost had asked him who the man with the Virginia accent was. He knew Charles had a funny accent and was not a native New Englander, but was it just coincidence that he happened to hail from the place he was now headed?

He wondered how long Charles had been working for his uncle. Uncle Raymond had obviously been to Virginia on at least one occasion. Did he hire Charles when he had last visited? Or was it just coincidence? And what were those papers Charles hastily pushed under his blanket? Clearly, something was not right.

It took him a while to fall asleep, but sometime during the night, he dozed off and when he finally did wake up, he could see a sliver of daylight coming through the parted curtain in the window.

He rolled out of his bunk and stretched. Lacing up his brogans and throwing his cloak over his shoulders, he walked out into the cold, blustery morning. He met the major coming up the stairs.

"Master Isaac, good. You are awake. Come, we dine in the captain's cabin."

He followed the major around the rear smokestack and passed a couple of weary firemen, their faces covered in ash and soot. The ship was enshrouded in a dense fog that forced the captain to reduce speed to avoid a collision in the shipping lane. Every so often, the ship's foghorn would blare out into the mist as a warning to nearby ships.

"You must have been extremely fatigued to sleep through that noise," the major said, opening the door to the captain's cabin. "You even slept through the excitement at Jersey City."

"Yes, sir. I slept like a log," Isaac mumbled.

The captain was a short, stocky man of about fifty years, with thick calloused hands and a ruddy, weathered complexion. His beard was fire red, speckled with gray. He reminded Isaac of a leprechaun. Major Frost introduced him as Captain Mayberry.

They sat down around a small table. Isaac greedily dug into a bowl of gruel and then wolfed down a few slabs of greasy bacon, washed down with a mug of piping hot coffee.

"Aye, boy, easy with the speed that ye devour thet grub or yuh gonna have an aching belly!" the captain said with a chuckle.

"Sorry, sir, I forgot my manners," Isaac replied, but the old sea salt seemed not to care.

"Laddy, the good major here tells me that yuh gonna be comin' back this way in a week or so. Well, I'm gonna refit the old *Pegasus* in Norfolk and she should be ready tuh blow steam about the same time that you are comin' back. I can save yuh cabin for yuh if yuh wire me when you are coming. Might have tuh wait a few days for the old ship tuh pull anchor. Her boilers need a good cleaning."

The boy nodded, cramming the last slice of bacon into his mouth.

"Aye, sir. I would like that. If I can find a telegraph office in Norfolk, I will be certain to let you know. Thank you, sir."

Isaac forced down the rest of his coffee and by the time that they had finished breaking their fast, the fog had lifted, bathing the *Pegasus* in the bright morning sunlight.

The captain took him for a tour of the boiler room and showed him the intricate workings of the massive paddle wheels, which he was much impressed with. The rest of the day he spent out on the deck, talking to Major Frost and avoiding Charles as much as possible. The Italian woman and her daughter had disembarked at Jersey City, thankful for Isaac's benevolence. Unable to find him, they had left a message with one of the Italian sailors who expressed thanks to Isaac on their behalf.

Charles attempted to soothe the animosity between them, but his ingratiating behavior did not fool Isaac. He was now convinced that his uncle had misjudged the man's character.

"That is Norfolk," the major said, pointing to lights in the distance. "We will be docking soon."

Isaac was leaning on the starboard rail feeling the cool breeze on his face. It was late, and he glanced up at the hazy band of the Milky Way stretching across the night sky. He was feeling apprehensive. At least on this vessel, he had a friend in the major. But once he departed, he would be forced to deal with Charles on his own, along with any other problem that might arise. He wondered if he were up to the task.

The Norfolk docks were bustling with activity as Isaac stepped off the *Pegasus* with his duffel bag thrown over his shoulder. Charles was no longer acting as his porter, which was fine with him.

He shook hands with the major, who gave Charles a threatening look before disappearing into the crowd. It was busy on the quay, people shuffling and elbowing others as they hustled about trying to find loved ones. Or perhaps they were merely anxious to get home after being cooped up on a ship so long. Drunk sailors staggered about looking for coin so they could continue to imbibe. One of them stumbled headlong into Isaac. He could smell the rum oozing from him.

"Watch where yuh goin', boy. Next time I'll beat the stuffin' out a yuh!"

Isaac ignored him and continued to move forward with the crowd. He looked behind him for Charles, but he had disappeared! Panicked, he desperately searched the throng of people but the big man with the bald head was nowhere to be seen. He had abandoned him.

Isaac's hunch had been right. Charles was not to be trusted. He was carrying all the important papers Isaac needed to bring Joy back with him. Isaac backtracked, heading toward the *Pegasus*, hoping to catch a glimpse of the servant, but nothing. The crowd had dispersed somewhat on the quay, but people were still milling about. Before long, the only people who would be out and about would be pickpockets and drunks.

He started to worry but managed to calm himself. All was not lost. He still had the money his uncle had given him. He would find a hotel and get a room. In the morning he would seek out a coach to take him to Jericho Plantation. He would explain to them the situation. Also, he still had a friend in the city. Major Frost would help him if he became desperate.

He stumbled out into the gaslit streets until he found himself standing in front of a large building built in the Roman style. He had seen depictions of similar buildings in books. It was a towering edifice, fronted by six fluted granite columns. He quickly identified it as the Custom House.

He headed up the steps and ducked behind one of the columns, crouching down in the darkness. He took off one of his brogans and stuffed half of his banknotes in his sock. Before he left Massachusetts, he had also sewn a hidden pocket in his wool cap which contained a few dollars. It was a precautionary measure. It wouldn't do to be robbed; he would then be destitute and have no way of hiring a coach the next day.

He thought about finding a place to lay low for the night, but in the end decided to try and look for lodging. That had been his plan to begin with.

Slinging his duffel bag over his shoulder, he headed back out into the streets. He had no idea where he was going, except that he was looking for an inn. He passed a bank and then found himself in what appeared to be some sort of market. Vendors had started to close shop for the night, but he managed to find an apple cart and paid the shopkeeper a penny for two apples, which he quickly stuffed in his duffle bag. It was then that he noticed a man lurking in the shadows, watching him. Or was it just coincidence that it was the sailor he collided with earlier? He felt a knot in his stomach.

"Could you tell me where I might find lodging for the night?" Isaac asked the apple cart vendor, a short man with a bushy brown beard and beady eyes. The man cocked a thumb toward a side street.

"Take Union Street. Couple blocks you'll see the National Hotel. It's across from Colley's shipyard. Can't miss it."

"Thanks!"

Isaac hurried along. He knew he was faster than this man stalking him, but he did not know the layout of the streets and there was no way of telling if the man might duck into an alley and cut out in front of him somewhere.

He could see his breath as he attempted to put distance between himself and the man. At one point, he turned around and was relieved to see that the man had seemingly been swallowed by the darkness.

Finally, he arrived at the hotel. The gas lamp in front of it was flickering as if it couldn't make up its mind whether to stay lit or not. He entered the lobby and approached the front desk. There was no one there, so he rang the bell. He heard somebody shuffling around in the adjacent room and then boards creaking under footsteps. A middle-aged man appeared wearing a monocle on his left eye. He had a curled moustache and greasy black hair that he had swept back on his narrow pate like a tide going out to sea.

"What can I do for you?"

"I...I'd like a room for the night, sir," Isaac said, out of breath. He could feel his heart beating rapidly in his chest. He had run the last two hundred meters or so.

"You got coin, boy?"

"Yes, sir."

Isaac reached into his pocket and threw a silver dollar down on the open register book.

"You're lucky. We have one bed. You'll have to share it."

"Share it? I want my own bed," Isaac replied, throwing another silver dollar down on the book.

The clerk eyed the second coin and stuffed it in his pocket. He turned and examined the keyboard behind him, first choosing one and then changing his mind and selecting another key from the top of the board. Isaac could see at least a dozen keys hanging on nails. The man was a liar.

"Room 230, second floor," the clerk said, handing the key to Isaac. "Breakfast is at sunrise in the dining room. Sign the ledger, please."

Isaac dipped the pen in the ink and signed his name neatly on the first empty line before handing the pen back to the clerk, who wrote down the room number next to his name. Without saying another word, the clerk returned to the small room behind the desk.

Isaac picked up his duffel bag and as he was getting ready to climb the stairs he turned and saw his stalker loitering outside the glass door. The boy shuddered. No matter. He was safe now. He had a room, a warm bed, and would worry about what he would do in the morning. He was plumb tired.

Craig R. Hipkins

He crawled into his bed and was sound asleep when a noise awakened him sometime during the night. At first, he was disoriented, not remembering where he was. He started to sit up when he felt pressure on his chest and something cold, like steel, touching the nape of his neck. A wave of panic overtook him as a large, calloused hand covered his mouth to stifle any screams.

"Make a sound, boy, and I'll slit you ear to ear," the foul-breathed voice whispered.

It was the sailor from the quay. Isaac was in trouble.

Chapter 6

saac sat on the edge of his bed as the sailor dumped the contents of his duffel bag onto the floor. Some clothes fell out, along with a slim leather-bound book, which the scoundrel examined and then stuffed into a pocket in his jacket. He scattered the remainder of the boy's belongings with a sweep of his hand, finding a comb, a needle, thread, and the apples he had bought in the marketplace, sending one of them rolling across the floor.

The sailor lit a candle and held it up in front of his greasy, unshaven face. He smiled, showing a set of broken yellow teeth. "Where's the coin? Yuh got it hidden somewhere, don't yuh? I know yuh got it! A boy dressed as fine as you has silver and bank notes somewhere. Yuh betta tell me or it won't go well for yuh!"

He was in Isaac's face, the halitosis causing the boy to wince and turn away.

"I...I spent the last of my money on this room," Isaac lied, his voice quivering. "Please...I have nothing but what you see on the floor."

The sailor kicked Isaac's duffel bag across the room and then noticed his cloak draped across the chair. He grinned and began rifling through the pockets. He pulled out the paper that Major Frost had given him, quickly examining it before losing interest and throwing it on the floor. When he found nothing else in the cloak, he shook Isaac's dress jacket and a few coins fell out of a pocket. He scooped them up and held them out in the palm of his hand. "Yuh lied to me!"

Shoving the coins into his pocket, the sailor placed the candle on the table next to the bed and advanced toward Isaac with rage in his eyes, the sharp blade held out in front of him. "I'm gonna cut yuh!"

Isaac reacted quickly. With one swift movement he pulled the quilt up and threw it over his attacker's head, temporarily blinding the drunken lunatic. This gave the boy enough time to flee. He quickly darted out into the hallway and crashed headlong into a man and woman who had just arrived at the top of the staircase. Isaac got the worst of it, tumbling to the carpeted floor.

"Whoa! What the devil, boy? Why in such a hurry?"

The man had grabbed Isaac's arm and pulled him to his feet just as the sailor came flying by them down the stairs and into the lobby. He dashed out the front door, disappearing into the night.

"That...that man! He robbed me!" Isaac screamed, pointing toward the door.

The man was still holding Isaac's arm. He was tall, well-dressed, with a thick walrus moustache that hung over his lips, threatening to consume his granite chin. He turned to the woman. "Stay with him."

The man went bounding down the stairs and he, too, disappeared outside but returned a minute later, out of breath.

"Gone! The constable needs to do something about these rascals. I'll talk to him in the morning," the man said, rubbing his square chin. "Where are your folks, boy?"

"I don't have any folks. I'm by myself."

They escorted Isaac back to his room and saw its disordered appearance.

"What did he steal?" the woman asked. She was rather young, with long, flowing brown hair. He told them the thief had only managed to get away with a few nickels, and a book before he fought him off. The man squatted down and picked up the large hunting knife the thief had dropped.

"Looks like you got the better end of the deal, son," the man said, feeling the texture of the blade. "This is a Bowie knife. Worth a might bit more'n' a few nickels and a book."

Isaac was sitting on the edge of his bed. He was dressed in his nightshirt and felt a little embarrassed in front of the young woman. She was gathering up his scattered belongings and putting them back in his duffel bag.

"My name is Cole Davidson, and this here is my daughter, Noelle. Where are you headed, boy? And what you doin' in this port town by yourself? You ain't from around here. From your accent, I'd say you was a Boston Yankee."

Isaac nodded. "Yes, sir. I am Isaac Barker from Boston. I am headed to Jericho Plantation in the morning. My uncle has purchased a young slave's freedom, and I am going to take her back with me," he said. He noticed Cole's eyes widen.

"Well, well. Isn't this a coincidence. We, too, are headed to Jericho Plantation. In a few weeks, Noelle here is to be married to young, Joseph Jericho, Wil's oldest boy."

It was the girl's turn to speak. "It wouldn't be Joy that you are coming for, would it?" she asked, exchanging a hurried look with her father.

"Yes, ma'am. Joy is her name. She is Esther's sister. You know her?"

She giggled. "Of course, I know her. She is a wild one. Wait until you meet her! I am surprised Wil is selling her. By the way, how do you plan on getting down there?"

Isaac shrugged. "I plan on hiring a coach."

She chuckled again. "Nonsense! You will come with us. Father owns a dining car with the Seaboard and Roanoke Railroad. You will travel as our guest. We will be in the next room if you need us."

Isaac thanked them, relieved that he would no longer be alone for the next part of his journey. When they were gone, he checked under the mattress to make sure his money bag was still there. It was. He breathed a sigh of relief.

Isaac examined the sailor's knife. It was a nice one. He wondered where a scoundrel like that had acquired it. Stolen, no doubt. He would get a sheath for it and at the first opportunity have his initials engraved on the handle.

There was no more sleep for him that night. He spent it awake, tossing and turning and acutely aware of every little noise that seemed out of the ordinary. After all, the sailor would be missing his knife and might try to recover it.

In the morning, he met the Davidsons in the dining room for a quick breakfast. He did not feel much like eating but forced down a few mouthfuls of egg and melons. When they were done breaking their fast, Cole Davidson hailed a coach that took them to the railyard where they boarded a private car at the end of the train next to the caboose. It was a small car, with curtains in the windows, a few bunks, and a table with four chairs. The locomotive was soon rolling down the gauged track, blowing thick black smoke from its funnel.

"Father owns a large stake in this railroad. He had this car custom built," Noelle said, seemingly trying to impress Isaac, but the boy remained stone-faced.

Isaac looked out the window at the scenery rolling by him. Field after field of tobacco. He could see men and boys laboring in the fields, slaves who worked from sunup to sundown. They looked miserable but, at the same time, resigned to their tedious work.

"They are preparing the fields for the spring planting," Noelle explained. "Sometimes, this is done in the winter also, but around here they start early."

"It looks like brutal work," Isaac remarked.

"Harvesting is worse. It happens during the hottest months of the year. But the slaves are used to it. It is what they were born to do," she remarked, examining her fingernails. "Father says slavery is a necessary evil, don't you, Father?"

Cole had leaned back in his chair and closed his eyes. He mumbled something in the affirmative. Isaac was not convinced. To him, it was inhuman and appalling to see these people laboring under an overseer with a whip, ready to find the first person who sulked from his work.

The train rumbled along, every now and then sounding its horn at a crossing. It was about twenty miles to Suffolk and when the locomotive finally pulled into the station it was mid-morning.

Isaac followed his two traveling companions onto the platform. A young, well-dressed man of about twenty-five years was standing there waiting for them. Noelle ran to him and embraced him. Joseph Jericho was well-built with a healthy, ruddy complexion. He kept his black beard trimmed short, but it was his wide, crooked nose that stood out. He was the caricature of a prize fighter. Isaac took an immediate dislike to him. Cole stepped forward and shook his future son-in-law's hand, the two men engaging in pleasantries.

Isaac stood off to the side, feeling rather awkward and out of place. He did not know these people and really did not want to know them. He only wanted to go home. After a few minutes of small talk, Joseph finally noticed the boy standing aloof.

"And who is this boy?" he asked, barely making eye contact with Isaac.

"That, my dear Joseph, is Isaac Barker from Massachusetts," Noelle said, taking Joseph's rough hands and turning him toward the boy. "He is here to buy Joy from your father."

Isaac swallowed nervously as the bearded young man sized him up. He concluded that young Jericho was definitely surprised to see him.

"Where is Charles Braxton, boy?" Joseph asked, finally addressing him.

At first, Isaac was confused. He never knew his servant's last name. He also thought it odd that this man would ask him about a mere servant. Did they not know that he was acting as his uncle's agent? "I...I don't rightly know, sir. He left me on my own at the docks in Norfolk."

A slight smile crossed Joseph's bearded face. Isaac thought it almost diabolical.

"Well, no matter," Joseph said. "The coach is waiting. Yuh will have to ride on the buckboard with old Moses. Thar is no room for you inside. Y'all have a nice talk now."

Moses was a thin, elderly man, with white whiskers and a shiny bald head. He helped Isaac up onto the buckboard which had a comfortable spring seat. Moses sat on a pillow. He gave the boy a sideward glance before whipping the horses into motion.

The carriage was almost as nice as his uncle's back in Massachusetts but lacking the new paint. Isaac was gazing out at the barren fields. There was nobody working them, which he thought rather odd. Every now and then he would steal a glance at the driver, who seemed to have a perpetual grin on his old, weathered face. Isaac wondered what he had to be happy about.

"First time at Jericho Plantation? I never done seen yuh afore," Moses said, breaking the silence.

"Yes, sir. I am here to bring Joy back to her sister in Massachusetts," Isaac responded.

Moses looked surprised, wiping his nose with the back of his large leathery hand. He slowed the horses down as they approached a crossroads and turned the carriage down a hard packed gravelly road.

"I ain't no sir. Yuh can jest call me Moses. What's yuh name?"

"My name is Isaac, sir."

Moses rolled his eyes and pointed to a large house far in the distance.

"That thar is Jericho Plantation. Thar is not another one like it for miles around. I was born in da kitchen, some eighty winters ago. Yes, siree, my momma was peelin' carrots and lay down on the flo' and here I come. They say I popped out of her, looked around some, and then tried tuh crawl back in!"

Moses let out a loud, boisterous laugh and slapped Isaac playfully on his knee. The boy cracked a smile as Moses began to tell him a little bit about the place.

"Are you a slave?" Isaac asked.

"Oh, no, sir. I bought muh freedom goin' on ten years now but got nowar else tuh go. Got muh own little cabin next to the stables and that's where one day the good Lord Jesus will take me up in his arms!"

The plantation house was fast approaching. It was a magnificent brick structure with two large wings jutting out from it. Two ancient live oaks stood on each end of the house, appearing like sentinels.

Isaac squinted into the sunshine, which felt good on his face. They turned onto a smaller lane made of flagstones and flanked by two neat rows of cypress trees. There was a stillness in the air that seemed to make the noise of the carriage's wheels louder as they grated along the stone driveway.

Moses stopped in front of the great house and climbed down. There was no one there to greet them, which Isaac thought rather odd. He slung his duffel bag over his shoulder and followed everyone inside, all except for Moses who took the carriage around back to the stables. A tall man wearing a white suit appeared in the foyer, seemingly having emerged from a wall. Isaac thought that he looked like a younger version of Moses. He was undeniably related to the older man, whether a son or a much younger brother. Without saying a word, he retrieved the Davidsons luggage, which Moses had left on the front porch.

Isaac felt awkward. He was left with Joseph as the Davidsons climbed the marble staircase. At first, Joseph seemed to ignore him. Isaac watched him pour himself a glass of wine from a canter and guzzle half of it before realizing Isaac was even there.

"I suppose yuh want to see Joy," Joseph said, using his big hand to wipe away a few drops of wine that had spilled down on his beard.

Isaac nodded. "Yes, sir. My uncle told me all I needed to do was sign the pertinent papers on his behalf and get them—"

Joseph held up a hand and waved at him to stop. "No need to explain yuh situation to me, boy. Ah don't need tuh see any papers and ah surely had not spected tuh see yuh alone. I spected tuh see yuh with Charles Braxton."

Isaac was confused and it must have shown on his face because Joseph shook his head and poured himself another drink.

"I...I don't understand," Isaac said. "Charles was my servant. Why would you need to see him?"

Joseph took a sip of his drink. "Boy, yuh don't get it, do yuh? No, course yuh don't. Yer but a pawn in the grand scheme of things."

Isaac suddenly felt sick. He had no idea what was going on. He only knew that somehow, in some manner, he had been tricked by someone to make this trip to Virginia. He suddenly wished he was back in Massachusetts with Thomas.

Anywhere but here. Joseph approached him, holding the wine glass gracefully between his thumb and index finger.

"Boy, Raymond is naïve. He might be a great man up thar in Boston with all of them bluebloods and educated snobs, but he got a one-track mind it seems. Yes, siree, all he cares tuh think about is them damn tobacco-pickin' slaves and thar damn freedom."

Isaac was nervously chewing on his lip. Just as Joseph was about to say something, the tall man in the white suit appeared again. This time he was holding a bag that Isaac immediately recognized as belonging to his servant.

"Master, Charles Braxton has arrived," White Suit said with a slight bow.

Joseph wet his lips. He appeared not at all surprised by this revelation. "Well, don't jes stand thar. Show him in, Lucias."

Lucias disappeared, and when he returned, the bald servant was with him, carrying the small portfolio that contained all the documents Isaac needed to legally obtain Joy's freedom. The boy stepped forward and when Charles noticed him, his face turned white.

"What's he doing here, Joseph?"

Joseph Jericho was grinning and waved his half-empty wine glass in front of him. "Now, Cousin Charles, the question should be, why did yuh abandon him on the dock?"

"What did yuh want me tuh do? Murder 'im and throw 'im in the Elizabeth River? What do we need him for? He has served his purpose. I have the documents we talked about right here in this portfolio."

Isaac felt his heart racing. He was involved in something that was beyond his understanding. Whatever it was these two scoundrels were up to, they had obviously hoodwinked his uncle. Was his uncle aware Charles was Joseph's cousin?

Somehow, he had to get away from this place. He had to contact his uncle. But how? He was miles from the railroad depot. He could walk there and catch the train back to Norfolk, but would they just let him go?

He listened as the two men bantered between themselves as if he weren't even there. Finally, he could take it no more. He had to find out what was going on.

Just as he was about to confront the two men, he happened to glance out into the next room and his eyes caught a glimpse of a young girl. She was thin—in fact, almost emaciated—of

African descent, with narrow features and big brown, doe-like eyes. She was wearing a blue checkered dress and had a white kerchief tied around her scalp, covering her hair, if she even had any.

Her eyes briefly darted his way and when they met, she quickly disappeared into another part of the room. He heard a door close, followed by light footsteps in the hallway. Isaac knew who she was. She was the sole reason for him being here. She was Esther's sister, Joy...and he had to talk to her now.

Chapter 7

Isaac stared out through the foggy glass of his bedroom window. Lucias had taken him there and told him dinner would be served at five o'clock. He would be back to get him. Until then, he was to remain in his room. He heard the skeleton key turn in the lock as added insurance of his compliance. Isaac protested, of course, but Joseph had insisted it must be this way.

He wondered where the Davidsons had gone. Did they know how he was being treated? He was now a prisoner at Jericho Plantation, and he did not know why. He suddenly felt homesick. He wished Bandy was here, and Thomas. He had never felt so lonely. He wondered what Bandy was doing. Did his friend miss him?

He stood up and checked the door, pulling on the knob. He had already done this when Lucias first locked him in, but it was frustrating to sit around doing nothing. He checked the window, but it was nailed shut. Even if he could open it, he would have to drop twenty feet or more and risk breaking a leg—or worse, his neck. And then what? A four- or five- mile walk into Suffolk on the only road he knew. They would surely find him missing and catch up to him somewhere on the road. He would have to take to the fields, but then he would risk getting lost.

He thought about Joy. Maybe she could help him? After all, she was the reason he was here—at least, that was his uncle's reason. He pulled out the silver pocket watch his uncle had given him shortly before he left. It was not even four o'clock. He still had an hour before Lucias would return. It was maddening!

He had just sat back down on his chair when he heard a key jingling in the lock on his door. He quickly stood up, expecting to see Lucias but was surprised to see the young kerchief-wearing girl he had seen earlier. She gave Isaac a furtive glance before walking over to his nightstand, where she picked up his water pitcher. She then started to leave.

"Wait! Where are you going?" Isaac asked.

She stopped and turned toward him, a blank expression on her face. "To get you some water."

She started to leave again, but Isaac stopped her. "Don't you know who I am?" the boy asked. If anyone knew anything, surely this girl did.

"No. Why do I care who you are?" she replied. "I was told to get you some water and that's what I am doing."

"But wait!"

She shut the door on his face, locking it behind her. He stomped his foot in frustration and slammed his fist on the wall so hard some plaster came with it. He returned to the window and peered out. He saw Moses come out of the stable carrying a bucket and a brush and disappear behind one of the smaller tool sheds.

There was nothing to do but wait. The girl, Joy—if that was who she was—would be coming back with the water. He waited, but she never reappeared. It was Lucias who returned with the water. He set it down on the table and was about to leave when Isaac confronted him, barring his way by standing in the doorway.

"Where is the girl that came up here and took that pitcher?" he asked.

Lucias looked genuinely puzzled. "Sir?"

"The girl with the kerchief. Is her name, Joy?"

"Ah. Yes. Joy has a headache. She has gone to lie down. She is not feeling well, and Mrs. Henrietta is taking good care of her."

"Mrs. Henrietta? Who is she?" Isaac asked.

Lucias once again appeared confused. "Why, she is Master Wil's wife. Come now, follow me. It is dinner."

Isaac followed the tall man down the marble staircase into the dining room. Joseph was sitting in between Noelle and her father. They were sitting across from a young teenage boy and Charles, who was eyeing his former charge with disdain. At the head of the table, sat a middle-aged man with beady blue eyes and a bull-like, white-bearded face.

There was nothing good about Wil Jericho. He exuded pure evil, and Isaac could sense it. He felt his heart racing again and his palms were sweaty with anticipation. Lucias motioned for Isaac to sit in the empty chair between Charles and the teenage boy who was looking at him in a sheepish sort of way.

"Well, well! Looky here. Our whole family here together," Wil exclaimed loudly. "Well, all 'cept Henrietta, who dotes on that little imp like she is blood.

Joseph snapped his fingers loudly. "Now, come on, Papa. Yuh know how Mama always wanted a daughter. Well, now, the little girl, Joy, gives her that illusion. By God, jest let her be."

Isaac glanced at Charles who was reaching across the table for a plate of cold cuts. He grabbed a few slices of ham with his grubby fingers and threw them on his plate. He also snagged a biscuit and began munching on it before anyone else had even picked up a knife or fork. It wasn't long before everyone followed the bald man's lead and soon nothing could be heard but the chomping and mashing of teeth. Isaac watched as Wil Jericho cleaned the stringy meat off a chicken leg, letting the grease dribble down his beard. He noticed Isaac staring at him and let out a light chuckle, waving the stripped bone in the boy's direction.

"So, Cousin Isaac, Ah do hope that Jericho Plantation is livin' up to your expectations. Wouldn't want kin folk back in Boston thinkin' us Virginians are crude and rustic, now. We aren't all bumpkins, yuh know."

Isaac swallowed nervously. He was not sure he heard him correctly or if he had just imagined it. "Cousin?"

Wil dropped the chicken bone on his plate and picked up another one, ripping off the skin with his yellow teeth. He began to laugh, throwing spittle across the table. Isaac turned his head in disgust.

"Uh-huh. Yuh didn't know you and Joseph are second cousins? Our good uncle conveniently left that part out, didn't he? Ashamed of his good bred southern relatives. Yuh see, momma, God rest her soul, was yer grandaddy and Uncle Raymond's kid sister. Why do yuh think he came down here two years ago? Yuh see, momma was dying of cancer, and he wanted tuh see her before she gave up her mortal cares."

Isaac turned white. He had no idea these people were his relations. It was appalling to him. He felt like screaming and running from the house but was glued to his seat as if some invisible force held him tethered to it. Everyone was staring at him as if he were a freak in some carnival sideshow. He thought about his uncle back in Massachusetts and suddenly felt a rage boiling up inside of him. Why did he not tell him the Jerichos were related to him? Was it because of their differing ideologies? He silently cursed his uncle. How did the old man think he would not find out?

He felt someone patting him on the back. It was Charles, who was smirking. He was obviously taking great delight in Isaac's discomfort. Isaac wondered how he fit into the equation. Was he related to him? His question was answered by Charles himself, who seemed as if he might be reading the boy's mind.

Leaning over, Charles whispered into Isaac's ear, "Don't worry, boy. Ah'm not your relation. Ah'm but the poor nephew of muh Aunt Henrietta. Yuh see, your generous uncle hired me as a sort of butler, but I have higher ambitions."

It was all a nightmare. He stood up and started to leave the table, but Charles grabbed his wrist and pulled him back down in the chair.

"Where are yuh goin', boy? Where are your table manners?" his former servant asked. Charles's face was inches from his, and he tried pulling away but the tyrant twisted his arm. He could smell Charles Braxton's foul breath, reeking of pork, and he suddenly felt sick to his stomach, the bile rising in the back of his throat.

Wil Jericho clapped his hands and pointed to Charles. "Release the boy, Charles. I think he knows his place."

Charles let go of his arm. Isaac felt like crying but somehow managed to hold back the tears. He did not want to give these sadists the satisfaction. He looked over at the Davidsons, hoping to find support, but they merely sat there looking stone-faced. He would get no help from them.

"Now," Wil said, raising his wine glass toward Isaac, "let us all have a nice Sunday dinner. One big happy family. A toast to Cousin Isaac!"

"Cheers! Cheers!" Joseph yelled, mockingly. Everyone raised their glasses.

Charles leaned over, poured some wine into Isaac's pewter goblet, and held it up to the boy's lips. "Drink!"

Isaac had never tasted wine before, and he turned his head away in disgust, but Charles was not to be trifled with. He grabbed the boy by his jacket collar and pulled him forward, forcing the goblet up to his lips.

"Drink, by God, or you'll be sorry!"

Isaac tasted the sweet port wine as the brutish man held him fast and forced it down his throat. He gagged as some of it dribbled down his cheeks and onto the chair. When the goblet was empty, Charles refilled it and repeated the process. Joseph began clapping, as did his fiancée. Noelle nudged her father to join in on the fun, but Cole was indifferent to the boy's plight. He merely sat there chewing on a slab of ham.

Isaac finally managed to work his way free from Charles's tight hold, but when he stood up to try and get away, the former servant backhanded him across the face. Isaac landed on his back on the rug, his hands covering his face. Charles reached down and lifted him to his feet.

"What in the name of the Lord Jesus is going on in here!" came a crackling voice. A woman had entered the room. She was middle-aged and rather on the plump side, with her blonde hair tied back in a bun. She had piercing blue eyes.

Isaac caught a glimpse of her as Charles forced him back into his chair. She was pointing toward Charles who had his, thick leathery hand clamped down on the top of Isaac's head.

"Let that boy alone, Satan, or the Lord Jesus will smite you on the day of judgement!"

This comment caused a cacophony of laughter from around the room, all except for the timid teenage boy who still sat with his head down, poking at a piece of ham on his plate with his fork. Wil stood up and waved his butter knife at his wife.

"Now, Etta, we jest havin' a little fun with Cousin Isaac, that's all. The boy is gettin' to know his family," Wil said with a chuckle. "Now, go tend to your little pet, unless yuh want tuh join us fer a bite."

Once again, the room erupted in laughter. Isaac felt his head spinning. The wine had burned the back of his throat, and he glanced around him at the sea of heads laughing and pointing at him. Their faces were muted except for the soulless eyes and wine-stained lips and beards with grease dribbling down them. Charles let go of his head, and Isaac made his move. He could stand no more of this insanity.

He staggered out into the hallway but the whole house seemed to be spinning. He felt a wave of nausea as bile made its way to the back of his throat. They all followed him out into the hall as he found the staircase.

"The Lord is coming!" Henrietta screamed. "The day of judgement is upon us! Mark my words! It is almost here!"

Isaac hit the stairs running, but his legs felt weak and wobbly, his head a myriad of thoughts and confusion. Spinning around, he felt as if his mind had left his body. They were mad! All of them. His last thought before passing out on the steps was that somehow, in some manner, he had to get out of here.

Chapter 8

Awareness was slowly coming back to Isaac. It was dark, he knew that much. He was on his bed with a light blanket covering him. There was a candle on the nightstand, its flame flickering from side to side. His head was throbbing. He was sickened from the wine and his throat felt parched.

He sat up on an elbow and looked around. He could see the outline of a person sitting in a chair beyond the flame of the candle. He could tell by the profile that it was the young girl with the kerchief. Was she Joy? He was almost certain of it.

Suddenly, a wave of nausea hit him. He leaned over the side of the bed and vomited into a bedpan the girl had the foresight to place there. When there was nothing left but an empty gag reflex, she took the pan and left the room, leaving him half hanging off the bed.

She returned a few minutes later with a clean pan. He watched silently as she poured him a glass of water from the pitcher and moved her chair next to the bed. He was sitting up with his back resting against the headboard.

"Drink this. It will get rid of your headache. You are dehydrated," she said in an almost mechanical voice.

She held the glass to his lips, and he took a few sips.

"Drink as much as you can, but not too quickly," she added, after he had stopped sipping.

He drank slowly until the glass was half empty. She then placed it on the nightstand next to him. He wiped his mouth with the back of his hand while he studied her angelic face illuminated by the candlelight. He couldn't help but notice she was pretty, but something about her demeanor bothered him. She seemed to be preoccupied with something, as if her mind was wandering to other places.

"Are...are you Joy?" he finally asked, finding his voice.

She nodded, without looking at him.

"I'm Isaac. I know your sister, Esther."

Her eyes finally met his, and they seemed to widen. She wet her lips with her tongue and leaned forward with her thin arms resting on her knees. "You know Esther? How?"

"My uncle...you know him. He purchased Esther's freedom, and he has sent me here to purchase yours. You are going to leave with me. I'm taking you away from this horror."

She was staring at him with a look of astonishment. "You have been tricked," Joy said. "They will never let me go. Mother Etta treats me like a daughter, but I am nothing more than her little pet. She told me to come here to attend to you. I saw what they did to you."

Isaac listened to her and realized she was right. Somehow Wil Jericho had managed to manipulate Raymond Barker, but he still could not figure out why. None of this made any sense. Was it out of sheer vindictiveness? He didn't think so. There had to be a reason.

He was feeling better, though his stomach was still churning. His headache had lessened, and he was finally getting to talk to Joy. Somehow, they would come together and make sense of all this.

"Joy, you might be right. But I do not understand why I was sent down here. Obviously, my uncle thought he was doing the right thing. I...I don't understand."

Joy handed him the glass of water. "Drink the rest of it. You will feel better in the morning. I have to go. Mother Etta requires me to read her to sleep every night."

She stood up and started to walk away but Isaac called out to her.

"Joy, wait. I will get you away from this madness."

She turned around and he could see her gaunt profile, the kerchief tied around her scalp. He sensed sadness. Without replying, she left him alone and headed out into the dark corridor.

****

A light under Mother Etta's door told Joy she was still awake. Henrietta Jericho had an almost obsessive fear of fire and would never leave a candle burning while she slept. Joy knocked lightly on her door and entered the room, where she found Mother Etta sitting up on her bed, flanked by half a dozen fluffy pillows.

"Ah...there you are, little one. I do hope the boy is feeling better. That nephew of mine belongs with the devil's minions, and one day he will be claimed by them! Are you ready to read from the Good Book, my dear girl?"

Joy nodded but her mind was not on the Good Book—or any book, for that matter. She was preoccupied with what Isaac had just told her, and as she read from Psalms, her audience knew something was not right with her. Joy was reading without inflection. She lacked the passion in her voice she normally used when reading. Still, she read on as Mother Etta listened. When she had finished, Joy shut the book and placed it on the nightstand.

"Joy?"

"Yes, Mother Etta?"

"Kiss me on the cheek, my daughter. I am tired and wish only to sleep now."

Joy leaned over and kissed the old woman's perfumed cheek. She could smell the port wine on her breath and was repulsed. She always hated kissing her, as she did not feel it was genuine, even though Mother Etta had always taken good care of her and protected her somewhat from the harsh realities of some of the other slaves on the plantation. However, she remembered how the old woman had treated her sister, Esther, on the day Raymond Barker had taken her away. Mother Etta had felt betrayed. She had chased Esther out into the yard and beat her with a hickory switch before Raymond bundled her away to safety. Joy had no doubt she would be treated the same way if she were somehow able to secure her own freedom.

Mother Etta's eyes had closed, and Joy blew out the candle and crept silently from the room. She thought about going back to check on Isaac. She wanted to know more about her sister and Raymond Barker's attempt at buying her freedom. She started in that direction but stopped when she suddenly heard voices coming from the small library at the top of the staircase. Silent as a cat, she stepped into the shadows next to the grandfather clock and listened.

"I say we take that boy and dump him in the swamp somewhere. I tell yuh he knows too much," a voice said. It was Charles. Joy felt a sickening knot in her stomach.

"Now, cousin, let us not be too hasty. We need tuh think this out," Wil Jericho replied. "Yuh had a simple task tuh do: steal Uncle Raymond's will from his safe, bring it hea' and use Joseph's forgery skills tuh altuh it in our favuh."

Charles cleared his throat. "Wil, don't blame me. By God, I got the will. It was your idea to concoct the whole story 'bout sellin' Joy!"

Wil snapped his fingers. "Lower your voice, cousin. Yuh want everyone else in this house tuh know our business? Now, how would it look you comin' down here by yerself not two hours after they find Uncle Raymond dead in his bed. Don't

102

yuh think it would look a might suspicious? They jest might decide tuh do an autopsy and mebbe find that he died by arsenic poisoning. Now, wouldn't yuh, disappearin' like a damned ghost be the main suspect? I provided us with a convenient excuse for your sudden departure. Now, I admit, we got us a problem. The question is...what tuh do with the boy? If he disappears, there will be talk. Might bring suspicion on us. Too many people know he is here."

Joseph interrupted his father. "We will have tuh make it look like an accident, Papa. Day after tomorrow, I'll take 'im out in the swamp with Elijah on the pretext of lookin' for one of the coon hounds. Quicksand will take care of him and when it's done, we'll cause a big ruckus and have the sheriff come out and help us dredge it. With Elijah as a witness, it'll look like a case of a dumb city boy makin' a fatal mistake."

There was a pause and Joy decided she had heard enough. She slipped away, her stocking feet tiptoeing silently across the carpeted hallway. She had to warn Isaac.

****

Joy entered Isaac's room so quietly, he did not even hear her until she was nearly upon him.

He was sitting on the edge of his bed with his head buried in his hands.

"Isaac," she whispered.

Startled, the boy's head shot up. He was surprised to see her. She sat down in the chair next to his bed, folding her hands in front of her. He could see her brown eyes, almost glass-like in the moonlight streaming in from the window.

"I...I know what this is all about," she said quietly. "You are in great danger and must leave this place."

Isaac leaned closer to her. He had almost forgotten about his wine-induced sickness. "Tell me!" he said.

She held a finger up to his lips. "Quiet! If they find me in here talking to you, it will not go well for either one of us."

The boy nodded, and Joy related all she had heard. A knot tightened in Isaac's stomach. Of course. It all made sense now. Once again, he was an orphan. He thought about Thomas. What would happen to him? There was Esther. She would take care of him until he returned...if he returned. His uncle Raymond was dead. Charles had murdered him. He could hardly believe it.

Isaac thought about his options. They planned on drowning him in the swamp the day after tomorrow. His gut instinct told him to pack his things and leave right now, taking Joy with him. It was suicide to linger at this place any longer. What if they changed their mind? The Jerichos were evil, and Charles Braxton was a murderer. To think he was related to these monsters was appalling to him.

"Joy, we have to leave tonight," he said.

She shook her head. "No, Isaac. We will need help to leave this place. If we take to the road, they will catch up to us. Even if we take to the woods, they will hunt us down with the bloodhounds. There was a field slave named Munger who attempted to escape about three years ago. It was shortly before Esther left. They caught him in the swamp. It was terrible. His legs and feet were all cut up by thorns, but his agony had only begun. Wil Jericho had all the field and house slaves come in to watch Munger's punishment. They hanged him from a sturdy pin oak and lit his writhing body on fire. He was still alive, choking to death, his skin boiling as the Jerichos and their minions laughed and joked. I can still smell the stench of burned flesh. It...it was terrible, Isaac."

Isaac was gazing at her, his mind filled with the horror of it all. "Joy, how far is it to the train station in Suffolk? Is there another way besides the main road? It cannot be more than a few miles. I have money."

"Lucias sits by the door. He would not let us pass. All the other doors are latched and bolted shut. I have an idea, but we will need the help of Moses. He takes the wagon into Suffolk every Monday for supplies. We might be able to convince him to let us stowaway under the canvas in the back. It is our only chance. That will get us to Suffolk, but from there we will have to find another conveyance to get to Norfolk."

Isaac brightened up. "We will take the train from Suffolk. Like I said, I have money and—"

She interrupted him. "They would never let me on the train with you. Everyone knows me there. Mother Etta takes me there on occasion. The Jerichos have friends everywhere. I...I am afraid I would only slow you down. I...I think you need to go without me."

He was about to respond when the sound of a creaking board outside the door struck terror in both youths.

"Quick! Under the bed!" Isaac whispered.

Joy was like a cat springing to action. She easily slid on her belly under the bed. Isaac watched nervously as the door to his room opened. He could see the silhouette of large man standing in the doorway as his eyes adjusted to the dark. A dim candle the man was holding, illuminated the room in a soft glow. A wad of spit mixed with tobacco hit the floor. The man crept closer toward the bed. Isaac prayed that the man did not hear them talking. If he did, they would be in big trouble.

Isaac looked up at the bloated, bearded face of Wil Jericho and feared they had decided to end things for him earlier than they had planned. The man's toothy grin was menacing. For a few seconds, he merely stood there, holding the candle in front of Isaac's face. He then began scratching his head with his tobacco-stained fingers, before reaching down and grabbing the boy by his collar, pulling him to his feet.

Wil Jericho was a big man and Isaac tried not to show fear, but inside he felt himself trembling, knowing the brute could kill him with one powerful blow from a clenched fist. He glanced down at his duffel bag on the floor. Inside was the Bowie knife that he had taken from the sailor back in Norfolk. The Davidsons knew he had it but had obviously forgotten about it or didn't think it was worth mentioning to Wil Jericho. If he could get to it, he might have a chance--- that is, if this monster had ill intentions.

He could hear a dog baying at the full moon—or was it a wolf? The noise seemed to distract Wil and he went to the window, peering out into the moonlit darkness. Isaac quickly bent down and retrieved the knife, slipping it under his pillow just as Wil turned back toward him.

"Boy, I just received a telegram from our good Uncle Raymond. Seems his ole heart has grown cold. He has reneged on the sale of the little negress."

Isaac swallowed hard. He knew this was a lie.

"Seems he wants yuh tuh stick around a bit down here and learn a man's work. Yuh'll help old Moses in the stable," Wil said, as he tousled Isaac's hair. "Work the city boy outta yuh. See yuh at breakfast, boy...and don't be late."

Isaac watched the big man stalk out of the room. "He's gone," Isaac whispered to Joy. "Let me go to the door and listen to make sure."

Isaac tiptoed to the door and opened it a crack, peering into the hallway. He could see the glare of Wil's candle get dimmer as he disappeared down the staircase. Returning to the bed, he reached under it and grasped Joy's hand, pulling her out. He noticed she was massaging the top of her head as if she had some discomfort.

"My...my uncle said that there was a doctor in Boston....He might be able to help you."

He helped her sit on the edge of his bed. For a brief second, her eyes seemed to sparkle with hope and then she lowered her head.

"Mother Etta took me to a doctor in Richmond. They believe it is a tumor. There is nothing they can do for me."

Isaac sat down next to her. "You don't know that. Maybe he is wrong. Uncle Raymond told me this doctor in Boston is the best. He is experimenting with operations on the skull and has had some success. You...you must come with me. You will be free! This...this is wrong. This whole place, wrong."

Joy looked up at him. "I...I better go. I'll talk to Moses in the morning. Maybe he can help us," she said.

Isaac was beaming. "Then you are coming with me?"

She nodded. "Yes. God willing,"

Without saying another word, she tiptoed across the floor and was gone. Isaac stared at the closed door. His throat still felt dry, and he poured himself a glass of water from the pitcher. He lay back on the bed, pulling the blanket up around him and touching the ivory handle of his Bowie knife. He felt reassured knowing it was there. He hoped he wouldn't have to use it, but if anyone tried anything, he would be ready. He wondered how he would conceal it in his clothes. He did not have a sheath. Maybe Moses could help him.

With his mind rambling, he tossed and turned for what seemed an eternity before finally succumbing to the merciful bliss of sleep.

Chapter 9

Isaac stuffed the Bowie knife in his heavy cloak and slipped on his brogans, lacing them tightly. Nervously, he made his way down the marble staircase into the dining room, which he found unoccupied, except for the teenage boy who sat nibbling on a crumb cake. He looked up and nodded when Isaac entered. Isaac responded warily with a quick nod.

"Ah'm yuh cousin. Name's Elijah," the teenage boy said.

Standing up, he held out his hand and Isaac shook it. The boy was a sickly looking youth with pasty-white skin topped with a mop of unruly brown hair. Despite being nearly two years older than Isaac, they were roughly the same size.

"Where is everyone?" Isaac asked, glancing around.

"Momma is sick, and Pa and muh brother, Joe, had tuh go help the neighbors with huntin' down a rabid coyote. They said it killed a couple of thar goats."

Isaac felt a wave of relief come over him. But then the image of Charles Braxton floated across his mind. "What about Charles Braxton?"

Elijah had sat back down and was playing with some cold scrambled eggs with his fork. "He's upstairs, drunk in his bed. Ah'm sorry what they done tuh yuh, Isaac. I don't like it."

Isaac grabbed a plate and helped himself to some scrambled eggs from a big dish on the table. He was famished, and thirsty. Elijah poured his cousin a cup of coffee. Isaac gave him a quizzical look and thanked him.

"Pa told me to go ride the fields and make sure the slaves aren't slackin'. Sort of disagreeable tuh me. He also told me tuh show yuh to the stables. He wants yuh tuh help old Moses. How come yuh come down here? They don't tell me nuthin' 'cept your folks died in a fire. I didn't even know I had cousins up in the North. What's it like up thar? I hear tell it is really cold."

Isaac shrugged, spooning a chunk of scrambled eggs into his mouth, and washing it down with a sip of coffee. "There will be snow soon and the lakes freeze over," he replied. "Good ice fishing with tilts." He caught a glimpse of Joy passing by in the hallway, heading for the front door. He wondered if she was going out to talk to Moses.

"I'd like tuh visit the North one of these days," Elijah said, interrupting Isaac's train of thought. "Been tuh Washington once. Saw President Buchanan pass by in a coach near the White House. He winked at me."

Elijah chuckled and forced another bite of biscuit into his mouth. He was eyeing Isaac and seemed disappointed when his comment didn't get any reaction from his cousin. Isaac was too preoccupied with what Joy might be doing, and he had sort of tuned out the older boy.

"When will your father and brother be back? Did they say?" Isaac asked. He hoped Elijah would not be suspicious of his motive for asking. He liked the boy, but still did not trust him.

"They won't be back until after lunch. It's a bit of a ride to the old Cooper place. Then they gotta track that coyote. Might be a bit later than that."

"I've never seen a coyote before," Isaac replied.

"They're ugly scavengers. Pa shot a bigun' last winter. We think it mighta been a hybrid, part wolf, mebbe but don't rightly know fer sure."

"Maybe so," Isaac mumbled. "I think I'll go out and see how I can help Moses."

Elijah stood up. "I'll come with yuh. Gotta get Betsy and take her fer a ride out in the fields."

The two boys walked out into the cool gray morning. It was overcast, and Isaac hoped that it would not rain. They found Moses in the stable, tending to one of the horse's shoes. He looked up and smiled as they entered.

"Elijah. I suppose yuh come tuh take Betsy out. She's bein' a bit stubborn this mornin', so I'd take her nice and easy."

Elijah rubbed the chestnut's mane and noticed that Moses had already saddled her.

"Thanks fer puttin' the saddle on her, Moses," Elijah said. "Yuh know I can do that now. I'm not five no more."

The old man chuckled. "I know that. But I also know that yuh don't like doin' what yuh pa makes yuh do. So don't give me no hard time about it, young 'un."

Elijah playfully tapped Moses on the back and then easily lifted himself up into the saddle. With a quick salute he was gone. Isaac watched him until he was out of sight, the horse kicking up dust in the road behind him. He quickly turned to Moses, who had picked up two pails and handed one to him without a word. Moses started for the well. Isaac followed the old man out into the yard. He wondered to where Joy had run off. He had seen her heading for the front door. Now would be the best opportunity for them to hit the road. With the Jerichos gone, the only one he had to worry about was Charles Braxton. He thought about the Davidsons. They had seemed friendly enough at first but had taken part in the revelry at his expense the day before—at least Noelle had. It was obvious they could not be trusted.

When they arrived at the well, Isaac became impatient. "Sir, have you seen Joy this morning?"

He could not wait any longer. If they were going to leave, they had to do it now.

Moses demurred, holding a finger up to his lips.

"Eyes be always watchin' at Jericho Plantation," he whispered. "Look busy and we will talk in the stable."

After filling the pails, they hauled them back to the stable and dumped the water in a trough in one of the stalls where a large black stallion stood watching them.

"I go to Suffolk 'bout noon," Moses said quietly. "Joy come by a little bit ago. She told me what happened. I gotta say that it is sho risky what you plan tuh do but I admire yuh greatly for it, sonny."

Isaac was chewing on his fist, his mind turning in circles. If they waited until noon there was a chance that the Jerichos would return and then the whole plan would be shot.

"Is there any chance of leaving now?" he asked.

"Can't. Gottsta finish feedin' the horses and goats. It's always been like this, and if I change it up someone might get suspicious."

As they were talking, Isaac glanced over at the mansion and broke out into a cold sweat. Charles Braxton was standing in the portico holding a steaming cup of coffee in one hand and what appeared to be a pistol in the other. He looked particularly menacing with a red wool cap covering his bald head. He was staring at the stable, as if he might be pondering whether to walk in that direction. Isaac cautiously stepped behind one of the support timbers. He didn't think Charles had seen him, but he wasn't going to give the man another opportunity to abuse him. He knew full well what he was capable of and did not want a confrontation.

Isaac noticed a small cream-colored dog crossing the yard, sniffing the ground, following a scent. It stopped close to the well when suddenly a loud shot echoed into the gray morning. The dog yelped and seemed to jump a few feet into the air before turning over and lying still in the brown crab grass. The smoke was still hovering around the muzzle of Charles Braxton's flintlock pistol, and Isaac could see a smile of sadistic pleasure on the brute's face.

"Mangy mutt!" Charles said. He turned around and disappeared back into the house.

"That...that monster!" Isaac exclaimed, sickened by the sight. "He...he just killed that dog for no reason!"

Moses removed his cap and, despite the coldness of the morning, wiped the sweat from his brow. He placed a comforting hand on the boy's shoulder. Isaac's face was red, and he tried to fight back tears. He loved animals and to see one brutally slaughtered in front of him was almost too much for him to understand. He had to get away from this madness.

"I must find Joy. We need to leave, Moses!"

The old man gazed at the boy. "Joy will be here at the wagon at noon, sharp," Moses whispered. "Now, until then we need tuh busy ourselves here at the stable. First, I need yuh tuh help me with the hogs out in the pen. Gotta fix the fence."

Isaac nodded, wiping a tear away. He was still looking at the dead dog and thinking about Charles Braxton's smug face as he walked away. Did the man have a soul or a conscience?

Moses shuffled over to a stout wooden toolbox and grabbed a hammer, some nails, and a board which he gave to Isaac who had followed him out into the yard. They crossed a bean field until they reached the pen which was situated next to a small stream. It was a large structure opened on one side with a stout fence to keep the swine from roaming free.

Isaac held one side while he nailed it to the post. They were almost finished when the boy happened to look toward the mansion. At first, he could not believe what his eyes were seeing. The pigpen was quite a ways from the mansion but it was open space. A man was half dragging someone across the yard, heading toward the stable. He immediately recognized the man as Charles by his red cap, but the smaller figure he could not make out until, with horror, he realized it had to be Joy.

He felt a rage take hold of him and his instinct told him to run— not away from the trouble, but toward it. He reached for his Bowie knife and before he could convince himself what he was seeing was not real, he had taken off in a sprint. Moses realized what Isaac was doing too late and hobbled after him the best he could manage.

Isaac covered the distance so fast he felt as if he had taken flight, his legs weightless and his breathing coming in short gasps. He stumbled one time, nearly impaling himself with his own knife, but he was back on his feet quickly and at the stable within a minute. Cautiously, he entered through the open doorway and heard a noise coming from one of the empty stalls.

"Don't fight me! Burnin' my toast! I'll teach yuh!"

The sound of a hard slap and a girl's cry sent Isaac into action. He flung open the stall gate to find a shocking scene. Charles was holding a riding whip high over his head, ready to strike Joy with it. There was a look of sheer terror on the young girl's face, and Isaac did not even hesitate.

"Let her go!" he screamed.

Charles turned around, his face a mixture of hate and surprise, his bloodshot eyes narrowing, cold and vicious. Here stood a man devoid of a conscience, a feral animal whose only ambition was power and profit. He was so shocked to see his former charge, he let go of his grip on Joy.

She immediately rushed away and ran over to Isaac who protectively pushed her behind him. The boy was nervously chewing on his lower lip, holding the Bowie knife out in front of him as if he were daring Charles to try and take it from him. He was holding the handle so tight; his knuckles had turned white.

"Well, look here. A real true bona fide hero!" Charles exclaimed.

The big man took a few steps forward, but Isaac lunged toward him with the knife, causing him to fall back.

"Give me the knife, boy, or I'll take it from yuh and rip your damn head off!"

Isaac was trembling, trying to keep his composure, unsure of what to do. Once again Charles took a step toward him, but Isaac waved the knife and he fell back again. Isaac could see the brute's eyes wandering around the stall, perhaps looking for a tool that he could use as a weapon. However, there was nothing but loose hay and piles of horse dung.

Charles's eyes were blinking rapidly. "Yuh skinny little waif! That damn uncle o' yours shoulda left you and your cry baby brother tuh starve in the streets! Give me the knife!"

Charles broke out into a fit of laughter. Isaac was horrified. The man was deranged! His eyes had murder in them, and Isaac knew one of them was about to die. He could run and most certainly distance himself from the older man, but that would leave Joy in his clutches, and she would fall victim to his wrath. There was no way he was going to let that happen. He took a brief glance behind him and could see Moses huffing and puffing, just entering the stable.

Noticing the boy's brief distraction Charles made his move and grabbed for the knife. Instinctively, Isaac lashed out and somehow managed to push the blade into the soft section of the big man's stomach, under the rib cage.

Charles let out an audible gasp, his eyes wide, a mixture of anger, pain, and shock, but the momentum kept him coming and he struck the boy. It was a glancing blow below Isaac's left eye and ear and would have been a fatal one had Isaac not managed to avoid the direct hit. Still, Isaac was felled by the punch and his attacker was quickly upon him, overpowering him and forcing him to the ground on his back with his large stubby fingers circling his neck. Isaac had dropped the knife and desperately attempted to extricate himself from the brute's hold but gradually felt his whole world becoming foggy.

Then, suddenly, his neck was free. He could see blood gurgling from Charles's mouth. His knife had been true! Isaac was still pinned under his former servant's great weight but only for a few seconds before a board came crashing down on the monster's skull. Charles fell over onto his side, his glassy eyes rolling back into his head. Joy was standing over the stricken man, holding the board and getting ready to give him another whack if he should stir.

Isaac fought to catch his breath, and Joy and Moses were soon by his side.

"Isaac, are you hurt?" the girl asked.

He had managed to sit up and was holding his sore neck. He was gradually regaining his breath. Joy had squatted down next to him and was examining the bruise forming under his eye.

"Oh...oh...You are hurt!"

Isaac was in survival mode. He looked over at the fallen form of Charles Baxter. The dying brute had turned over onto his left side, his hands instinctively holding the mortal wound in his stomach. A pool of blood was forming in the hard packed sand next to him. His breathing was shallow, then came in short gasps as a trickle of blood oozed around the corners of his mouth. With a final spasm, he ended his evil existence—a stain forever removed from the earth.

"Is he...?" Isaac asked, not able to say the word. He was in shock.

Moses was checking his pulse and said the words for him. "He's dead."

Isaac was terrified. He had just killed a man. He would hang for this. Or would he? Would they hang a boy of thirteen?

Joy disappeared and when she returned, she was holding a wet handkerchief she had dipped in one of the troughs. She held it up to the swelling under his eye. He winced. As she was tending to him, he looked up and saw a man standing next to the body of Charles. It was Lucias. The tall man was wearing his starched white suit and staring down at the corpse with a blank face.

Moses started toward him, holding his hands out in front of him. "Now, Lucias. Let me get these children away from here afore yuh go give the alarm. It was self-defense. The boy here was bein' attacked. This man here was no good...no good at all, Lucias, and yuh know it!"

Lucias glanced at Isaac, whose eyes were pleading with him. However, the soft-spoken butler said not a word. He turned and headed back toward the mansion at a brisk walk.

"Will he say something?" Isaac asked.

"Oh yes. My nephew is a cold one. He listens and knows everythin' that goes on at Jericho Plantation. He's gonna go snitch to the overseer out on the back twenty. We have tuh leave now. Hurry and go get yuh things, and I'll get the wagon ready."

Isaac struggled to his feet. He and Joy made a beeline toward the house.

When they returned to the wagon, Joy was dressed in her heavy shawl and had stuffed some edibles in a burlap sack. Moses told them to get under a large canvas tarp in the back of the wagon.

"Please, Lord, see these children are safe. I beseech thee."

Isaac peeked through a hole in the tarp. He could see the old man lift his weathered face toward the heavens and smile. For a brief second, the sun broke through the clouds, and he saw a tear run down Moses's cheek. Perhaps God was listening. He hoped.

Chapter 10

The bumpy ride into Suffolk seemed to take forever. Isaac and Joy were huddled together under the tarp, which was held down by a few sacks of grain. Moses was whistling a soft ballad.

At one point in the journey, the loud spatter of raindrops on the canvas gave cause for concern but they needn't have worried. The sky was breaking up and the heavenly rays of sunshine were soon shining down upon them. It was as if God had answered Moses's prayers. Still, it was unseasonably cold, with a bitter wind whipping across the barren fields.

The wagon stopped behind a small stand of willow oaks, the branches nearly stripped of their narrow yellow and brown leaves. Moses climbed down from the buckboard. Isaac could hear the crispy dead leaves crunching under his heavy steps. The tarp was drawn back, and the old man motioned for them to step down. Isaac leaped onto the ground and assisted Joy down. She pulled her shawl tighter around her shoulders to ward off the cool breeze, her lips pursed together in anticipation of what would happen next.

Moses beckoned for Isaac to follow him around to the buckboard where he fished around under the spring seat and grabbed a small canvas bag. Isaac was shocked when he reached inside and pulled out a small derringer pistol and set it down on the floorboard.

"Found it on this very road one day on muh way back from Suffolk. Not sure hows it got there, but now I know why I found it. There be some powder in the horn and a dozen balls and caps. I done loaded it, so all yuh need tuh do is pull back that hammer and pull the trigger. I pray tuh the Lord Jesus that yuh don't have tuh use it. Keep that powder dry."

Moses handed him the weapon and Isaac strapped it to his waist in the small leather holster next to his Bowie knife, which he had wiped clean of Charles's blood. He buttoned his heavy coat and looked up at Moses, whose brow was deeply lined with worry. The old man placed a hand on his shoulder.

"I leave her in your hands, young Isaac. This is as far as I go."

He pointed toward the elevated railroad bed that lay parallel to the road.

"Yonder is your road tuh freedom. Leads straight tuh Norfolk. 'Bout twenty miles as the crow flies. By now, Lucias has spilled the beans and they will be lookin' fer me and yuh all. When yuh hear the rail start tuh sing get off the track and intuh the woods or lie prone in the fields. It means a train is coming. They'll use the wire to message ahead. There'll be a bounty fer yuh capture. Trust no one."

Joy had silently crept up to them, her tiny footsteps making little noise in the carpet of leaves under her feet. "But what about you, Moses? If you return, they shall surely hang you," Joy said, her voice quavering.

Moses knelt in front of her, taking her small hands into his large, calloused ones. "Now Joy, don't go worrying none about old Moses. Old Moses knows a thing or two 'bout how tuh live and survive. I ain't lived these four score years and not learnt nothin'. Now you two run along and make haste. Yuh got a few hours afore they really start searching."

Joy reached out and wrapped her arms around the old man's neck and for a minute let her tears flow, knowing she would probably never see him again. Isaac thanked him and held out his hand which the old man took, and then, suddenly, the two youths were gone.

Moses watched them cross the field. Isaac with his duffel bag slung over his shoulder and Joy with her small canvas sack, wrapped in a wool blanket that she had tied with rope and carried on her back. When they climbed the steep embankment to the railroad track, they looked back and waved but Moses was already climbing onto the buckboard. They watched as the wagon rolled out of sight.

****

They walked in silence for a while, each one wrapped in their own thoughts. Joy felt like crying. Jericho Plantation was all she had ever known. She would miss Moses and even Mother Etta, who treated her kindly. However, she knew in the back of her mind that this day would eventually come. It was as if she had a premonition.

At Jericho Plantation she would always be a slave, at the subjective whim of whoever was master of the house. Now, at last, she was free, finally unencumbered by the tight yoke around her neck. She knew her time was probably limited, but if she could spend her remaining days with her sister, living free, it would be worth it. Also, there was always the chance of this doctor in Boston. What if he could do something for her?

And then there was this mysterious boy who seemed to have arrived out of nowhere. She had only known him for a day but felt like she had known him for a lifetime. He was brave and had rescued her against all odds from a tyrant that might have beaten her to death. He was walking a few steps ahead of her, his long hair sticking out from around his soft wool cap. She had never met anyone like him.

Isaac interrupted her train of thought. He stopped and held up his hand. "I think that I hear something."

She heard it, too— a soft but penetrating ring. There was a train coming!

He took her hand, and they hurried down the embankment and crawled into the switchgrass, making sure to keep low. After a few minutes the low ringing turned into a loud rumble and the unmistakable sound of train wheels as the flanges pushed against the rail.

Isaac looked up and could see a plume of heavy dark smoke towering into the sky as the engine rumbled by, trailed by its heavy load. It was a freight. Isaac had an idea but quickly dismissed it. Attempting to board a moving box car was tempting but extremely risky. He would be able to do it, but in her weakened condition, Joy would not. There was also the chance someone might see them and then the game would be up.

No, they would have to make the journey on foot.

When he deemed it was safe, they climbed back up the embankment and started again. He tried to remember landmarks from his train ride the day before. He wished that he had paid more attention. He didn't remember any large towns they'd traveled through, though there were houses and farms and places where the track snaked its way through a forest. There was no way they would make it to Norfolk today. It was almost noon, and at some point, they would have to find a place where they could conceal themselves for the night. That would take time.

He prayed that the rain would hold off, but the sun had once again hidden itself behind an overcast sky. To the northeast, the dark clouds looked ominous. They walked for what he determined to be about three miles into an area where there was forest on both sides of them.

Then the rain came.

At first it was a light mist, but it gradually increased into a cold sleet. They had to find shelter and find it fast. He remembered what Moses told him about the powder getting wet. He had stuffed the horn in his duffel bag and prayed the rain would not come down any harder.

He tried to get his bearings, racking his mind for places that might afford them shelter. If he remembered correctly, there was a large outcropping of boulders not far from where they were. They would head there and hope for the best.

Isaac noticed Joy shivering. The cold rain was coming down just hard enough to make it miserable. He caught her gaze and knew that they needed to get warm.

"There! Over there!" Isaac exclaimed suddenly.

She followed the direction of his extended arm and saw a bunch of rocks with trees growing out of fissures, a tangle of roots, shrubs, and granite. He took her hand and led her into the thick of it. They scrambled up a hill and then down into a series of large boulders.

Isaac had spent many nights in the woods and knew what he was looking for. He finally found it—an overhang, a natural shelter within the rocks. He helped her inside. It was a small area no more than five feet long. There was barely enough room for them to sit with their backs to the wall of granite behind them. It would, however, keep them dry.

"I will start a fire," Isaac said, disappearing in a flash to gather some wood.

A few minutes passed and Isaac finally returned with some deadfalls and rotting bark, which he stacked near his duffel bag. He made a couple of trips until he was satisfied that they had enough wood to last them for a while. He then fished in his bag for his tin of matches and built a small firepit, using stones to enclose it. Joy watched as he gathered some dry leaves and slabs of bark, building a pyramid of sorts. Soon, he had a warm blaze going that brightened their spirits.

They had found the shelter just in the nick of time. The sleet and rain were now coming down in a torrent, striking the dry leaves of the forest floor in crackling repetition.

"Well, at least this weather will slow the search party," Isaac said, adding some sticks to the flames. "Are you warm enough, Joy?"

She smiled. "Yes, Isaac. Thanks to you. I still haven't thanked you for...for saving me from that awful man. Why did you do it? You hardly know me."

He gazed at her, wrapped snugly in the wool blanket, and then turned back to the fire, poking at it with a sturdy stick.

"I...I saw him dragging you to the stable. I...I couldn't let him hurt you. I reacted, like it was someone else and not me making that decision."

Craig R. Hipkins

"Were you afraid?"

He sat next to her with his back against the cold granite wall and looked down at his feet.

"Yes…yes. I am ashamed to say that I was. But…but I couldn't help it. I mean…he was a lot bigger than me. I thought I was going to die and…and you, too."

She took his hand and held it.

"Ashamed? No, Isaac. There is no shame in being afraid and doing what is morally right. When I first saw you yesterday, I thought that you were just like all the other white folk I have known, but now I know different. You don't care about color, do you?"

He looked at her strangely, his bluish-green eyes blinking with the sting caused by the smoke from the fire. "Color? I…I don't understand," he said softly.

"My skin color. It doesn't matter to you, does it?"

He shrugged. "Matter? Why should it matter to me? I don't get cruelty. Why…I mean, why do some people have to be mean and evil? Why, Joy? There is too much wickedness in this world."

She smiled. "There is, but...there is goodness, too. I...I didn't think there was until today. Until you came."

He turned to her with a look of desperation. "But I killed a man. I...I didn't mean to kill him."

He buried his head between his knees. She could hear him sniffling and when he looked up, she could see his lips quivering and tears running down his cold, wind-burned cheeks. She sensed the conflict and agony that had taken possession of him. Here was a good soul who had been forced to kill out of sheer necessity, and it was eating his conscience alive.

Outwardly, he exuded strength, but he was still just a young boy taxed with the responsibilities of someone much older. She took her handkerchief and wiped away his tears and noticed the swelling under his eye had gotten worse. Without saying anything, she removed the blanket from around her shoulders and crawled out of the shelter.

"Where are you going?" he asked. But she did not respond. He watched as she dipped her handkerchief into a puddle and returned to the shelter. Squatting in front of him, she held the cold cloth on his bruise. He winced, but he let her act the nurse and he soon forgot about the reason that they were there.

"I don't think it is going to stop raining," he said.

"Oh, you are a pessimist," she said with a slight giggle. She playfully stuck her tongue out at him. He forced a smile. Suddenly, he felt a little better. If she could hold her head high under these dire circumstances, then he could, too.

"I stole some food from the pantry," she said proudly. "We won't starve."

Isaac still had his apples in his bag and some dried beef jerky. They would be okay in that respect.

She fished in her small sack and produced some biscuits and a few slabs of dry bacon. Taking a small paring knife she had stuffed into the pocket of her dress, she sliced the biscuits in half, placed the bacon between the two halves, and handed one to Isaac.

He was famished and greedily wolfed the food down in a few bites. He thanked her for it. It was getting late in the afternoon and the impending darkness sent him back out into the sleet to gather more wood. When he thought they had enough to last the evening, he settled back in, and the two youths watched the night engulf them. Somewhere in the forest they heard the howling of a coyote which lent an eerie uneasiness to the evening.

Isaac wondered if the search party was out looking for them. If they were, they would be wretched and miserable. He doubted it. Surely, they would wait until the weather was more favorable for travel. Or would they?

Either way, they were safe for the night. A posse would never find them here, nestled among the rocks. Even the smoke from their campfire was well hidden, the wind dispersing it into the firmament. Joy broke him from his silent musings.

"I am worried about Moses. I do hope he somehow manages to talk his way out of his involvement in helping us escape. Maybe Lucias won't rat him out."

Isaac was poking at the fire with a stick, causing a shower of sparks to fly up into the sky. "I hope you are right, Joy. Moses has lived there his whole life. Perhaps he can talk his way out of it, even if Lucias does rat him out."

For a short time, they sat in silence watching the flames lick up the wet smoky wood, each one caught in their own reveries. Finally, Joy broke the silence.

"Isaac?"

"Yeah?"

"What's it like? I mean, how is it where you live? I have never left Virginia. This life is all I have ever known."

He gazed at her, sitting, bent over, with her head resting on her knees. "Well, it's a lot colder up there, but you wouldn't know it from what we are feeling today. I am an orphan like you. Never really had any friends. Well, I...I do have one friend."

She looked interested. "You do? A boy or a girl?"

He shrugged and the hint of a smile crossed his face. "Well, you won't believe me if I told you."

She sat up and shuffled closer to him. "Tell me. I want to know."

He tilted his head back. "All right, but don't laugh at me. You promise?"

She nodded, leaning forward with her chin resting on her hands.

Isaac cleared his throat. "Well, I have this place... I go there often. Been going there since I was little. It's a pond. The water is always cold and clear. Sometimes it almost shines like God has polished it or something."

He made a motion with his hand as if he had a cloth and was shining the air. He continued, "There is wildlife in abundance, Joy. I see deer, wild turkey, fox, turtles, and birds everywhere. I know all the trees, lots of maples and oaks, hemlocks, and white pine and even an old chestnut. Sometimes I climb up into its branches, almost to the top!"

She interrupted him. "Isn't that dangerous?"

He shook his head. "Oh no. You see, it might sound strange, but I never worry about falling because the tree seems to protect me. If I slip, a branch is there to grab me. I know it sounds ridiculous, but it has always been like that. This...this pond is sort of my own little sanctuary. Everything is peaceful. We are all friends. It is like...like my own little heaven."

Joy became animated. "But your friend? Tell me about your friend?"

He smiled, a carefree look, his mind traveling back to the place. He then turned to her. "Bandy is his name. He is gray, with a pink belly and black spots with a band around his neck...He...he is a passenger pigeon," he blurted out. "I know you won't believe me. I never tell anyone. In fact, you are the first person I have ever told, though a few people have seen me talking to Bandy, but they just made fun of me. They think I am crazy."

He made a swirly motion with his finger against his temple to emphasize the "crazy" part.

"You talk to Bandy? And he talks back to you?" she asked, almost in a whisper, her mind a whirlwind of conflicting emotions.

Isaac nodded and lowered his head, embarrassed. "I...I told you that you wouldn't believe me."

Joy leaned closer to him, her eyes watering with tears.

"Well, you...you are wrong, Isaac. I do believe you. I...I want to go to this pond. It seems like it is a magical place! Will...will you take me there?"

The boy's face brightened. "You want me to take you there? Really?"

"Yes, unless you don't want me to go. I would understand. After all, it is your own personal spot," she said in a low voice, and then added, "I...I had my own spot, also."

He adjusted his position and sat cross-legged, folding his hands in front of him. "You do?"

"I did," she replied. "But I will never see that place again."

He was gazing at her with a look of attentiveness. "Tell me about your place. What's it like?"

She folded her arms, and he could see a smirk forming on her face and then she burst out laughing.

"What? What's so funny?"

She wagged her finger at him. "Now it's your turn to promise me you won't laugh."

He threw his head back and chuckled.

"I promise I won't laugh," he said with a wide smile. "But I must say that it is quite hard not to when you are laughing."

Joy gave him a playful tap on the arm. "That's because laughter is contagious," she said with a merry grin, showing her gleaming white teeth.

He scratched his ear and leaned forward. "Are you going to tell me or not?"

She nodded and suddenly became serious, almost meditative.

"Sometimes, I would go to this place... It was out in the pasture. I could still see the house, but it was far away. There is a spot where no grass grows. It...it is rather strange, a round spot about as big as the horse stable. Moses told me it was a faerie circle."

Isaac was puzzled. "What's a faerie circle?"

"Moses said that faeries are little elves or goblins and are associated with witches and the devil, but I don't believe it. He warned me to stay away from the place, but I never saw bad things there—only good things."

Isaac was mesmerized. "What kind of good things?"

"Well," she continued. "When you told me about Bandy, I ...I almost didn't believe it. I thought that I was the only one—"

She broke off in mid-sentence as if she were reluctant to continue. But Isaac prodded her. "The only one that what?"

She leaned closer to him and responded in a voice so low she was almost whispering. "Isaac, I...I talk to the animals, too."

Chapter 11

Isaac was stunned by the revelation. Never in a million years did he ever believe someone else had the ability to talk to animals of the forest. He thought he was all alone. Now he knew differently. This girl, whom he had only met the day before, conversed with them also. It was hard to believe but he had no reason to doubt her, just as she had no reason to doubt him.

"My friend is a white fluffy rabbit named Pink," Joy said. "I can talk to Pink about anything."

After she revealed her secret to him, they talked for hours about their past. Isaac told her about his family and how Thomas was the only one left. Joy, in turn, revealed that Esther was her only sibling. The sleet had relented somewhat but the wind had not abated. Isaac kept the fire going and made one more trip to ensure they had enough wood to last the night.

Eventually, exhaustion got the better of them. Joy had wrapped the blanket around their shoulders so that only their heads poked out. She was the first to doze off, her head resting on Isaac's duffel bag.

He checked his derringer, placing the lever on half cock and setting it next to him near his

Bowie knife. He felt reassured, having the two weapons handy. He prayed to God nothing would happen, but if it did, he was ready. Or was he?

It wouldn't be a lone man looking for them. They would have a posse out searching and possibly bounty hunters looking to make a quick buck. They would have to be careful. He wondered if keeping to the railroad was the wisest course of action. The pursuers would also have the benefit of traveling on horses.

Sometime after the witching hour, he must have fallen asleep. He awoke, shivering, and noticed that the fire had burned down to embers, the glowing remnants appearing like lighted windows in a village. He added some bark and sticks and used his cheeks like bellows, igniting the blaze again. Yawning, he checked his pocket watch. It was nearly four o'clock. He had been sleeping nearly four hours. He nudged Joy. She was sleeping soundly, and he hated to disturb her, but they had to get going.

Joy's head jolted up. She appeared confused and disoriented. When she saw Isaac, illuminated by the firelight, she seemed startled and instinctively scrambled away from him.

"Joy! It's me, Isaac."

Awareness finally came back to her, and she crawled back toward him. She sat next to him, rubbing the sleep from her eyes. She looked tired and scared. "I...I am sorry, Isaac. I was having a bad dream when you woke me. That...that awful man in the stable... He was back, and he was chasing me!"

He placed a hand on her shoulder, his eyes showing concern. "Well, you don't have to worry about him anymore. That bad man can't hurt you ever again."

She nodded. Closing her eyes, she began massaging her temples.

"Are you okay?" he asked.

"I...I am having one of my headaches and my vision is blurry."

He wrapped the blanket around her and helped her lay down, once again using his duffel bag as a pillow.

"I'll be okay in a few minutes," she said softly. "They always go away, but I need to keep my eyes closed."

He was worried. They needed to get an early start, but there was no way she could travel like this. The more miles they put in, the quicker they would get to Norfolk. He thought about Major Frost. He would help them, if only they could get

Craig R. Hipkins

there. Then there was the *Pegasus*. Captain Mayberry was saving his cabin for him. He was certain if they could reach Fort Norfolk, they would be out of Wil Jericho's reach.

As he was pondering these possibilities, he remembered the safehouse that Major Frost had told him about. It was in Portsmouth, across the river from Norfolk. They would head there first. If they left now, they might be able to reach it by early afternoon.

He strapped his derringer and knife to his belt and blew into his hands, rubbing them together. He had a pair of gloves but had given them to Joy. She needed them more than he did.

After nibbling on a piece of beef jerky, he was surprised to see her sitting up. She had removed her kerchief. He wondered why she always wore it. For the first time he saw her hair. It was cut short with black curls. She caught his gaze and turned away, quickly replacing the kerchief with her wool hat.

"I have a scar on the top of my forehead," she said. "I don't like people to see it."

He looked down at his feet, embarrassed for gawking. He felt awkward, not sure what to say to her, so he changed the subject. "We should leave, Joy. If you are feeling better."

145

She agreed. "I'll fold the blanket."

He helped her and when they were done, they extinguished the fire and carefully attempted to conceal any evidence that they had been there. A good tracker, he knew, would have no trouble finding their camp, but he doubted Wil Jericho or any of his cohorts had the skills his father had possessed and passed on to him. At least, he hoped not.

It had stopped raining, but the wind was still blowing and it was bitterly cold. They climbed the embankment and were soon back on the railroad tracks heading east.

Isaac was impressed with Joy's fortitude. For someone who was sick, she was able to maintain a quick gait, but he worried she might be overdoing it. He quickly realized she was not one to complain, despite her weakened state.

They walked into the daylight without any mishaps or meeting a single soul; not even a train disrupted their journey. It was shortly after the sun had risen when they came to the first signs of habitation. Small tenement houses sat nestled among the plucked rows of tobacco. Already the fieldhands were out, in the process of turning the soil, preparing for the next crop. They looked miserable and cold, dressed inadequately for the weather in their light cotton shirts and wool pantaloons. None of them were wearing coats.

Isaac felt bad for them, but Joy seemed to be resigned to their fate, ignoring them, and looking straight ahead. This life was all they had ever known. He asked her how they managed to keep sane, knowing they would never leave this way of life. She responded with indifference.

"They know nothing else. They were born to it," she said glumly.

He wondered why they did not all band together and revolt against their oppressors. He decided to keep this thought to himself. Joy, he understood, was well-educated, hence her predilection for books and her yearning for freedom. To others, these sentiments might be stymied by apathy and resignation to their lot in life.

After walking a couple of miles, they found themselves back in a forested region. Isaac felt better. The fewer people who saw them, the better off they were. Undoubtably, the search was on. He knew that Moses would try to mislead them, but he feared they might torture the old man into revealing their true direction of travel. He cringed to think of it.

He was about to take a drink from his canteen when he heard the ubiquitous ringing of the rail. Joy heard it at the exact same time.

"A train!" she exclaimed, nervously.

They quickly darted into the woods and took cover in a thick stand of chokeberry shrubs. The train was traveling slowly, much more slowly than the train that had passed them the day before and the ones that had passed in the dead of night. Anxiously, they awaited its passing, but the locomotive was chugging along until finally it came to a stop. Isaac told Joy to hunker down and crawled on his belly to a spot to better see what was happening.

Gazing through the thick foliage, he could see the cowcatcher of the locomotive, steam, and wispy black smoke drifting around it. The rest of the train was hidden behind a wall of pine trees. He had an uneasy feeling and he soon learned why.

A party of horsemen had appeared seemingly out of nowhere, the wet snouts of the sweating beasts breathing jets of steam into the frigid morning air. With horror, he noticed the bulky form of Wil Jericho, mounted, and looking formidable with his posse around him. Behind him, on a brown Morgan, rode Joseph. Isaac also recognized Elijah among the throng of horsemen on his small chestnut. The boy looked cold and miserable.

Joy crawled up next to Isaac, and he put a finger up to his lips.

"Do you think they saw us?" she whispered.

Isaac shook his head. "No, or they would have spread out all over these woods."

The engineer had stepped off the train and was talking to Wil Jericho. He was obviously incensed about something, and Isaac figured out why. The posse had stopped the train. He estimated that there were at least twenty men in Wil Jericho's posse, and all except for Elijah looked menacing and wicked.

"What's the meaning of this delay?" the engineer growled, pulling his cap off and waving it in Wil's face. "I have tuh deliver this load tuh the lumber yard in Portsmouth. It's already late and the shipper at the docks is gonna be mad as hell!"

Wil had dismounted and handed the engineer a slip of paper. "Judge Britton signed this warrant last night. A murderer on the loose, a boy named Isaac Barker. He got a little slave girl with him. Yuh see him yuh let someone know, yuh hear?"

The engineer, a short middle-aged man with gray whiskers, examined the warrant and handed it back to Wil.

"Hundred-dollar bounty tuh the man that brings him in," Wil said, emphasizing the point by sticking his finger in the engineer's chest.

Isaac trembled. He was now a fugitive and an accused murderer. Wil Jericho's influence would ensure that if he were captured, he would not get a fair trial. Indeed, if he even made it to trial. More than likely, there would be a lynching.

He was in serious trouble, and he now began to doubt their chances. Even if they made it to Norfolk, would Major Frost be able to protect him from those who sought to bring him to justice? Of course, it was all nonsense. He had been defending himself from a man twice his size and had saved a young girl from being whipped.

He wondered how Moses had fared. He assumed not too well. Their pursuers were on the right track. Moses might have been tortured and spilled the beans, but they could have guessed it as well. After all, the railroad was the most direct route to Norfolk, other than the main highway, which would have been heavily traveled. Anyone searching for them would naturally make a solid, educated guess that they might make use of this route.

The engineer disappeared and Isaac assumed he had climbed back onto the engine. He guessed right. The locomotive gathered steam and was soon rolling along again, leaving the posse to plan their next move.

Isaac prayed they wouldn't come their way. Although they were well hidden in the thicket, it was possible someone might catch a glimpse of a cloak or hat. He needn't have worried. He could see Wil Jericho talking to Joseph and another man, whom he called Carl. He was a large, burly man, with pork chop sideburns and a thick, bushy red moustache. He looked like a hard one. Joseph took Carl and half of the posse and set off toward the north. Isaac figured that they were heading toward the main highway that ran parallel with the railroad.

This left Wil, Elijah, and about ten other men who had dismounted. The father and son seemed to be having an animated conversation.

"Pa, ahm not feelin' too good about this," Elijah said, his voice cracking in the breeze. "I mean...I mean...Isaac don't strike me as the type that'd murder someone. Cousin Charles was tryin' tuh whip Joy, like Moses said and—"

Wil grabbed his son by the collar and backhanded him across the face. Elijah stumbled and landed in a heap next to his chestnut.

"You soft son of a bitch. Yuh finally found yuh mouth, didn't yuh! Yuh can't be from my seed. Your momma was whorin' around about the time you come around. Now get back on that mount and shut your mouth. I'll make a man of you yet!"

Elijah sat up and with the back of his hand wiped the blood away from his mouth. When he was slow in getting up, Wil became infuriated, reached down and grabbed him by his collar, hauling him to his feet. With a quick shove he sent the boy crashing into the chestnut. The beast, being skittish by nature, panicked and took off into the brush.

For a few seconds, terror took hold of Isaac and Joy as Betsy seemed to be heading straight for them, but at the last second, she veered to the south and instinctively headed in the direction of Jericho Plantation.

Some of the crasser members of the posse broke out into fits of laughter as Elijah stumbled in the direction of his mount, but his father collared him again and boxed his ear. The boy let out a pained scream.

"Now look what yuh done!" Wil's face was inches from his son's. The boy's eyes wide with terror. "I'm gonna take it outta yer hide, boy!"

Elijah struggled as Wil lifted his son off the ground and threw him down in the reeds and gave him a swift kick in the ribs, which sent him sprawling onto his back. Isaac pulled his derringer from its holster, capped it, and cocked the lever back, but Joy prudently stopped him from pulling the trigger by placing her hand on his and shaking her head.

Elijah struggled to his knees and held out his hands in front of him as the brute bore down on him. "Pa! Pa! Please!"

Wil's face was red with rage. "Sissy boy!"

The toe of Wil's boot connected with his son's chin, a glancing blow but enough to knock him unconscious. Finally, mercifully, three of Wil's cohorts, including Cole Davidson, managed to restrain the maniac.

"Wil, fer Gawds sakes, that's enough!" Cole bellowed into the wind. "You'll kill the boy."

Wil broke free of his handlers and spat a wad of spent tobacco onto the ground next to his fallen son, who was slowly regaining his senses.

"Looks like yuh got a long walk back tuh the homestead, sissy boy!"

He mounted his stallion and, with the rest of the posse, rode off toward Norfolk using the railroad right of way as a highway. Isaac and Joy waited for a few minutes until they were out of sight before emerging from their place of concealment and rushing to Elijah's side.

They found the boy sitting up, crying, his face bloodied from his father's assault. He was shocked to see them and at first afraid of what they might do to him. After all, he had been part of the posse chasing them.

"Don't shoot me! I...I didn't want tuh go with 'em!"

He was pointing at the derringer, which Isaac still held in his hand.

Isaac felt terrible. He quickly uncapped it, stuck it back in its holster, and held his hands out to show him he was unarmed. "No...no, Elijah! You have it wrong. I'm not going to hurt you. We saw what happened from that thicket over there."

The older boy relaxed and, leaning forward, he buried his head in his hands and began sobbing. "I'm sorry! I'm sorry! I...I didn't want tuh come!

They are planning on hanging yuh, Isaac. Yuh gotta get outta here, and Joy, too."

Joy squatted down next to him and placed a comforting hand on the crying boy's shoulder.

"They don't have us yet, Elijah," she said softly. "And they are not going to get us."

The wounded boy lifted his head, and they could see that he had been hurt badly. One of his eyes was swelling shut and his nose was bleeding. Isaac helped him stand on wobbly legs and threw his arm around his shoulder.

"Come on, we'll get you patched up," Isaac said.

They found a secluded spot in a stand of pitch pines away from the railroad, where they would be concealed in case Wil Jericho had a change of heart and came back to look for his injured son. Isaac did not think that he would. It was obvious he hated Elijah and abandoning him after a severe beating at least a dozen miles from home proved it. If, somehow, Elijah failed to show back up, he doubted the brute would lose any sleep over it.

Joy immediately took charge of Elijah's dire condition. She retrieved the canteen that Cole Davidson had considerately left for Elijah and used the water and a cloth to clean the boy's wounds, for which he was grateful.

He kept apologizing for his father's wickedness. She then ordered Isaac to make a small fire. After this was accomplished, she reached into her canvas sack and took out a container of dandelions, plantain, and chickweed. She mixed them together with hot water and created a poultice which she pressed into a cloth and wrapped it around Elijah's left eye, which was swollen shut. The girl possessed a delicate touch. She was a natural nurse and, Isaac thought, would make a good doctor.

"Where did you learn that?" Isaac asked, amazed at the girl's ingenuity.

"Esther taught me. Not sure where she learned it."

Elijah winced as Joy finished wrapping the cloth around his head and tying the ends together.

"What are yuh gonna do?" Elijah asked. "Pa telegraphed ahead. They are lookin' for yuh in Norfolk. Yuh can't go thar."

Isaac squatted down in front of his cousin, who had removed his cloak and shirt and was allowing Joy to inspect his injured ribs.

"Can you help us, Elijah? You aren't like them...I mean, your father and brother."

Elijah nodded. "They will kill me, but I...I don't care. How...how can I help?"

Isaac caught a quick glance from Joy, and she nodded.

"Can you send a telegraph message for me?"

"Certainly," Elijah replied. "Doc Stoner has one in his office in Suffolk. It will take me a while to walk there, but...but I was thinking of comin' with yuh. Yuh might need my help. I want tuh leave this place, Isaac!"

Elijah turned to Joy. "Joy, tell Isaac I ain't like them. I don't like none of it! People owning other people. Pa and Joseph always bullyin' people. It ain't right!"

"I know you aren't like them, Elijah," Joy said, "but Isaac's right. The best help you can give us is if you get a telegraph through."

Elijah wiped his runny nose with the back of his hand. "Awright. You jes' tell me who tuh send it tuh, and what the message is, and I'll get it through, if it's the last thing I do!"

Isaac placed a hand on his cousin's shoulder. "Elijah, send a message to Major Samuel Frost at Fort Norfolk. Tell him Isaac Barker needs his help. Tell him I am going to try and make it to address number two."

Elijah appeared confused. "Address number two?"

"He'll know what I mean. Can you do this for us, Elijah?"

The older boy struggled to his feet and held out his hand, and Isaac grasped it in friendship.

"You're damn right ah'll do it, cousin. If I cen find Betsy, ah'll be thar sooner than later!" he said, placing his hand gingerly on his head. "Dang it, my head's throbbin' like a locomotive run over it."

As he started from the thicket, Joy called out to him. "Elijah! You be careful!"

The battered boy turned around and waved, but then his countenance turned grave, and he returned. "Joy? It...it's about Moses."

She was gazing at him with glassy eyes as if she had a premonition of what he was about to tell her. "What? What is it?" she asked, her voice trembling.

Elijah's eyes were watering, and she could see tears rolling down his cheeks. "They strung Moses up, Joy... They strung him up!"

Joy became numb. She turned to Isaac who stood there, eyebrows lowered, lips quivering. No one said anything. Elijah backed away and then sped off toward the railroad tracks, turning around once. He was still crying.

Joy was still gazing at Isaac in disbelief. "You heard what Elijah said? They...they hanged Moses!"

Isaac had heard it, but he had been through so much over the last few days he seemed numb to everything. It was as if he were living in another reality. If he looked up at the sky and saw that it was full of angels and demons at war, he would in no way be surprised. He almost expected something like it.

Joy sat down in the grass and buried her head in her lap. She was crying. He, not really knowing what to do, did what any compassionate person would do. He sat down next to her and embraced her. Surprisingly, she reached around and hugged him back, letting the tears flow onto his shoulder. Though Isaac had not known Moses long, he, too, felt a tear rolling down his cheek. Moses was a good man and he had died so that they might live.

It was a while before they had regained their composure. In a few minutes they had extinguished the fire and then began to contemplate their next course of action. It was now risky to use the rails, but what choice did they have? They could traipse through the woods and fields but might get lost. Isaac had a good sense of direction and great wilderness survival skills for a boy his age, but he was in a strange land, with a girl under his protection, though she had proven to him she was certainly no damsel in distress. Still, she was sick, and she needed him. He came to a decision.

"Joy, I think we should hide ourselves and travel at night," he said. "It will be our best chance."

She nodded, her eyes still red.

He took her hand and they searched for a place of concealment. It would be a long day.

Chapter 12

The scent of burning cedar drifted through the air as Isaac and Joy hunkered down in a wooded gully within a stone's throw of the railroad tracks. They were well hidden. Isaac had taken thorough precautions but admitted to Joy they were taking a risk with the fire, albeit a small one. Still, someone might detect the smell.

The afternoon dragged along. Every cracking branch put Isaac on his guard. He kept the derringer loaded and at half cock. Joy had another episode and this one was longer than the one she had earlier in the day. Isaac had kept her as comfortable as possible next to the fire.

As nightfall approached, she felt much better, and they each ate a stale biscuit and a few slabs of bacon. It was a lean meal, but enough to give them energy to continue on their way.

They decided to use the railroad. There was a stillness in the air, and they would be able to hear the clomping of hooves if any horses approached. Isaac prayed Joy wouldn't have another one of her headaches. They seemed to come on with little warning and were debilitating.

A short time later, they passed by another small village of ramshackle houses. Isaac noticed a blacksmith's shop. The smithy, a raw-boned man with bulging biceps was hard at work at the forge and did not even notice their passing. The glowing light of a furnace left them longing for the warmth of a fire. With any luck they would be in Portsmouth by midnight.

They were about a mile past the forge when the sound of a neighing horse grabbed their attention and they quickly darted off the tracks into a stand of pines. They crouched down behind some brambles and waited.

A lone horseman came into view. He was a thickset man with a dark beard riding a large stallion, his menacing profile bathed in the moonlight. Isaac immediately felt a gnawing wave of fear in the pit of his stomach. The mounted man had obviously seen them. He had stopped and was peering in their general direction. He was most certainly a bounty hunter.

Isaac quietly pulled his derringer from his small holster and capped it. He felt Joy's hand find his free one. They glanced at each other nervously.

"Come on out, yuh murderin' boy! I done seen yuh along with that little slave girl yuh travelin' with!"

Isaac's pulse began to race. If he were older, he would pull this man from the saddle and pummel him for that comment.

"Let's go, boy! I ain't got all day now. Yuh come outta those bushes and don't give me no trouble and ah'll make sure yuh git a fair trial. If not, it ain't gonna go well with yuh!"

Isaac weighed his options. The way he looked at it, he had three. He could surrender—an option which he immediately dismissed. His second option was to fight it out with the man. He had the drop on him but surely the bounty hunter had a weapon of some kind on his person, almost certainly a revolver, which would neutralize his one-shot derringer. His third and final option was to sit still and do nothing. Let the bounty hunter come to them. There was a chance, albeit a slim one, that he would not find them in the darkness. He chose option number three and quietly whispered his intentions to Joy, who wholly agreed with him. They waited. They would let their pursuer make the next move.

Isaac swallowed and was nervously chewing on his lip. He could almost hear his heart beating in his chest. There was a prolonged silence between the bounty hunter and his quarry, each party waiting for the other to make a move. Finally, there was movement. The bounty hunter coughed into his hand and gently kicked the side of his horse sending it into motion. Beast and rider carefully descended the inclined railroad bank and headed on a tangent to where Isaac and Joy sat, anxiously awaiting their fate. They could hear the man's spurs jingling as he descended into the shallow ravine before slowly entering the woods.

It was pitch dark, but Isaac could see the silhouette of the bounty hunter who reached over and grabbed a coil of rope hanging from his saddle. Isaac correctly deduced he was going to try and use it as a lasso, should the two fugitives emerge from their place of concealment and try to make a run for it.

"Last chance, boy! Come on out, or ah'm gonna make it rough on yuh!"

With horror, Isaac could see the rider heading straight for them. They would be seen within a matter of seconds. The beast was snorting loudly as it took its rider through the shallow bed of pine needles that covered the forest floor.

Suddenly, Isaac had an idea. It was a long shot, but it just might work. Without saying anything to Joy, he leveled the derringer in the direction of the horse but not aiming at it. He fired. There was a loud report and the suddenness of the still night exploding with a flash had the desired effect.

The horse reeled back and, dislodging its shocked rider, took off, crashing through the brambles in a panic. The bounty hunter landed on his back in a thornberry bush, temporarily stunning him. Isaac quickly reloaded and capped his derringer and, with Joy, carefully approached the stricken man who was holding his leg and moaning in pain. However, when he saw Isaac and Joy, he quickly recovered and went for his sidearm, which was strapped in a holster on his belt.

"Make another move and I'll blow you to kingdom come!" Isaac exclaimed, standing a few feet from his fallen antagonist. He was pointing the derringer straight at the man's head.

The bounty hunter slowly held his hands up. He was no fool. Isaac had the drop on him, and he was in no position to offer any type of resistance—yet, a grin lit up his face. He had one card yet to play.

"That thar is a single shot yuh holdin' against me, youngster," he said with a slight chuckle. "Ah'm willin' tuh bet it ain't loaded."

"I'm willing to bet it is," Isaac responded. "But it's up to you whether you want to take that chance or not."

The bounty hunter quickly lost his smile. He had played his hand and lost. Even in the darkness, he could clearly see the percussion cap on the derringer's nipple.

"Now," Isaac said. "Remove your belt with that holster and throw it over there."

He waved his derringer in the direction he wanted the rogue to cast his belt. At first, the man hesitated but when Isaac took a step forward and aimed the weapon at his heart, he wisely did as he was told. The boy then handed the derringer to Joy.

"If he moves, pull the trigger."

Isaac then retrieved the bounty hunter's belt and removed the holster. He pulled out the revolver and inspected the cylinder. It was a five-shot Colt pocket revolver and it was fully loaded. Snapping the cylinder back into place, he stuffed the weapon back into its holster and attached it to his belt, adding it to his other armaments.

"My leg's broke," the bounty hunter said suddenly. "Yuh not jest gonna leave me here, are yuh?"

"You should have thought about that before you accosted us, scoundrel," Isaac snapped, looking down at the man's twisted leg which was bent back in an unnatural position.

Joy handed the derringer back to Isaac, and he opened his coat and stuffed it into his other holster. He now had two pistols and a Bowie knife and considered himself fortunate. This confrontation just as well could have gone badly for them.

The girl approached the hobbled man, being careful not to get too close. He was glaring at her with a look of hatred.

"You would compromise your principles for a hundred-dollar bounty?" she asked him.

"His kind have no principles, Joy," Isaac cut in, picking up his duffel bag and slinging it over his shoulder. "They lust for money and have no conscience."

The bearded man raised his arm and wagged his finger at Isaac.

"Yuh damn little murderin', thievin' Yankee! Conniving with slaves. Yuh don't know who ah am. I'm Walter Britton, son of the judge who signed your arrest warrant...I—"

Joy interrupted him. "You don't know the whole story. He was defending me and himself. He murdered no one! If he was a murderer, he would shoot you right now. Would he not?"

Walter coughed violently and looked beyond her to the boy who had removed his cap and was running his hand through his long flaxen locks.

"Come on, Joy. We need to get going," the boy said, touching her arm.

"His leg is badly broken, Isaac," she said. "It will need to be set before we leave. It shan't take me long."

Isaac shook his head. "It is too dangerous, Joy. He...he could grab you."

"Ah won't touch her. Yuh have my word as a gentleman," Walter said.

Isaac's eyes narrowed. "You are no gentleman, sir, but I reluctantly agree to her humane gesture of goodwill. However, you have my word as a gentleman that if any harm comes to her by your hand, you will deal with me."

Walter nodded. "I guess ah don't have much of a choice now, do ah, Yankee boy? Yuh cen shoot me raht between the eyes if I renege on muh word of honor."

Joy went to work. She quickly found a sturdy stick to use as a splint and had Isaac cut a few pieces of rope from the lasso Walter had been holding. She gave her patient a block of wood to chew on before she straightened his leg and used the rope to hold the splint in place. He grunted in agony as she performed the task, but she was soon done and stood up to admire her work.

"Your tibia is broken and possibly the fibula as well," she said. "Though I cannot feel a break there. It shall heal, though you will probably walk with a limp for the rest of your life. This cannot be helped."

The bounty hunter was staring at her with amazement. "The tibia? What in God's name is that?"

She shrugged. "It is the larger of the two bones in your lower leg."

Walter just stared at her, his eyes blinking confusion.

"She's going to be a doctor one day," Isaac said, throwing Walter his spare canteen, which was half full of water. He then turned to Joy, who had slung the blanket over her back. "Come on Joy. Let's get out of here."

They started to walk off, leaving the hobbled Walter to spend a dreary night in the darkness. It would take him a while to crawl up to the railroad bed and await an oncoming train he could flag down. By that time, they hoped to be in Portsmouth.

"Wait!" he called out to them. They both turned around at the same time to see him sitting up on his elbow.

"Why did yuh help me? Yuh didn't have tuh help me."

"Because we are humans, that's why," Isaac responded angrily.

Walter broke out into another coughing fit before finding his voice. "If yuh headed tuh Portsmouth, come in from the north. They done got the whole damn county out lookin' for yuh. Expectin' yuh tuh come in from the west. Tell yuh the truth, if I was you, I'd head east and hide out in the Dismal Swamp until this business settles down."

Isaac was perplexed. "Why are you telling us this?"

"You ain't no murderer, boy. I...I was dead wrong. I'm man enough tuh admit it."

170

Isaac approached him. Walter had sat up and was now resting with his back against a pine tree.

"I jest thought o' somethin'. If you insist on still headin' toward Norfolk, get off the railroad near the Marston House...a big brick place with Grecian columns about a mile from here. Cut across the field behind it till yuh see a small brook. There yuh will find a little-known path...some say an old Indian trail. It leads direct intuh Portsmouth."

Joy was rubbing her temples and Isaac noticed her discomfort. He helped her to sit down.

"What's wrong with her?" Walter asked. There seemed to be genuine concern in his voice.

"She gets bad headaches. It'll pass in a minute," Isaac replied.

For a few minutes, Joy sat with her head between her legs. Isaac felt helpless. Somehow, he could take down murderers and bounty hunters but when it came to something like this, he was at a loss. Finally, Joy seemed to recover, and she stood up as if nothing had happened.

Walter reached into his coat and pulled out a can of snuff and pinched some between his teeth and lower lip. He then rolled a cigarette and called for Joy. "Here, girl. When yuh feel a headache comin' on, smoke this. Always helps me."

He handed it to her and then motioned for them to move along.

"I'll leave your revolver with the provost marshal at Fort Norfolk," Isaac said. "That'll prove that I'm no thief."

Walter spat on the ground next to him. "Keep it. Yuh done won it fair and square. It's called trial by single combat, boy. Yuh won. Go on now. Git outta here and keep the doctor there from any mischief."

Isaac took Joy by the hand, and they headed back toward the tracks, leaving the stricken bounty hunter to wonder about his future. One that had just been turned upside down by an act of kindness.

Chapter 13

Marston House loomed heavy in the darkness. A dim light was shining from one of the upper windows, but otherwise it appeared dead and bleak, as if its occupants had decided to hibernate for the coming winter, which would soon be upon them.

Isaac and Joy had encountered no one since they had left Walter sitting under the pine tree. At first, Isaac was reluctant to follow the bounty hunter's advice, fearing a trap, but after discussing it with Joy, they decided the man had been sincere.

Joy claimed to be able to know when someone was being deceptive. She felt nothing of that with Walter and had told Isaac her feelings. They stopped at the well behind the house and filled their lone canteen, being very careful not to make any noise.

When they finished, they went in search of the brook Walter had mentioned. Joy was the first to see it. She actually heard it before she saw it, a low babble as the water softly cascaded over the smooth rocks forming a neat little pool. Joy thought this was definitely a place where faeries could dwell, and Isaac agreed.

"That trail must be around here somewhere," she whispered.

"Yeah, but where?" Isaac mumbled. "It's hard to see anything in the darkness, and I would hate to light a match. Someone might see it from the house."

They finally stumbled across it. A century-old willow oak marked its entrance. The path, covered with fallen leaves and pine needles, was barely wide enough for the two of them to walk side by side. Taking Joy's hand, Isaac led the way. He prayed they would encounter no one. If anyone were to be lying in wait, they would have no trouble hearing the crunching leaves under their feet.

Isaac looked up through the canopy of leafless branches above them and attempted to gain his bearings by way of the stars. He quickly found Polaris and determined they were heading northwest. By his reckoning, they were walking in the right direction.

It was a lonely night and somewhere to the east they could hear a hooting owl. Isaac kept a sharp lookout, imagining every shadow in the moonlight to be a possible bounty hunter. He kept his free hand on the butt of his Colt, feeling reassured by its presence. He only had five shots, but it would be enough to get them out of a scrape if needed. Then he would have to rely on the derringer which he had capped as a second option, should the Colt misfire. He prayed he would not have to use either one.

Joy felt comfortable despite the chill in the air. She had confidence in Isaac's ability to get them to this safehouse in Portsmouth. Thus far, he had managed to overcome every obstacle that had come their way.

She could, however, see the worry and heavy responsibility etched on her traveling companion's sallow face.

Isaac, on the other hand, felt a nagging, sinking feeling of despair within him. He admired Joy's outward coolness and her ability to keep him motivated despite the odds against them. However, he felt inadequate to the task that had been cast upon him by fate. Only a few weeks earlier he had been but a poor schoolboy. Now, here he was hundreds of miles from home, trekking through the Virginia wilderness with a sick young girl. He was also a fugitive from justice being pursued by bounty hunters and a lynching party of madmen. He thought about Bandy and Thomas, who was probably looking out the window of his bedroom at this very moment, hoping to see his big brother arriving home.

They had walked about a mile when Isaac detected a light ahead of them. It was a dim beacon, probably coming from inside a house. They were nearing the outskirts of Portsmouth, though they didn't know it. They stopped as Isaac gathered his bearings.

"From here on, it's going to get scary, Joy," he said glumly. He removed his cap and despite the chill wiped the perspiration from his forehead.

She was rubbing her round chin and turned to face him. "It's all right, Isaac. You aren't going in there alone. We will figure this out together."

He nodded, chewing nervously on his lower lip. He looked down at the ground. "I have this address, but I don't know how we shall find it, especially in the dark," he said uncertainly.

"I've been to Portsmouth with Mother Etta a few times," Joy said. "I am familiar with the main arteries coming in and out of the city."

Isaac reached into his cloak and pulled out the paper Major Frost had given him. He lit a match and held it over the scribbles. Joy's face brightened.

"I know the place! It is the new African Church. The old one burned to the ground a few

176

years back. I helped Mother Etta deliver some sheet music there last year!"

Isaac smiled, showing his gleaming white teeth. It was the first time she had seen him smile all day.

"If we can get there, I have no doubt that Major Frost will help us...that is, if Elijah can get that message through."

She nodded in agreement. "And if not, we can surely get someone at the church to get word to him."

He placed a hand on her shoulder. "Still, we must be careful heading into the town. There are sure to be scoundrels lurking about just waiting for an opportunity to capture us."

They started again and soon the trail disappeared and they found themselves on a narrow street lined with small clapboard houses. They detected the acrid, rotting smell of the marsh as they walked along the roadway. The houses were mostly dark, with an occasional light seeping through the inky blackness from an open window. This section of the town being poor and downtrodden, fuel for the fireplaces was likely scarce and used sparingly.

They kept to the shadows, but it wasn't long before they came up to the town proper, with its grid-like blocks of houses and buildings. Joy looked for landmarks and recognized a brick house with red shutters at which Mother Etta had stopped on their last visit. If she recalled correctly, the church wasn't too far from there.

As they turned a corner, they stumbled into a group of sailors and dock workers drinking beer and whiskey on the porch of a tavern. One of them, a young man with a thin black moustache and greasy hair, was sitting on the wooden rail and leaped down into the road in front of them. He was obviously drunk, and Isaac could see his glassy eyes fall on Joy. There was lust in them.

"Hey, fellas! Looky here! This boy here got himself a little girl!"

He stood in the road blocking their path with his hands resting on his hips.

"We don't want any trouble," Isaac said nervously, his hand on the butt of his Colt. He was chewing on his lip weighing his options. They could retreat or take a chance and attempt to pass by this blowhard and see what happened.

"Come on, Frank. Leave him be!" called one of the older dockers. "We goin' down tuh Sally's in a bit. There'll be plenty o' action around there, yuh dirty bird! That girl thar is a little young for yuh, fella."

Isaac and Joy had been forced to stop in the narrow roadway. Their only course of action was to retreat behind them or press onward past their antagonist. The man named Frank reached into his pocket and lifted a flask of whiskey up to his lips. He swallowed a mouthful, never taking his eyes off Joy.

"She old enough fer me!" he said with a hiccup. He stumbled toward them, his eyes glaring directly at Joy as if she were a piece of meat. He ignored Isaac, not even deeming him a threat.

Isaac, however, was having none of it.

"Come here, girl," Frank said, slurring his words.

The drunk docker reached for Joy with his large stubby fingers, but they never found their target. Seemingly out of nowhere, Isaac's fist shot up, connecting with the ruffian's chin, sending him sprawling on his back in the road. The boy could hardly believe it. He had been in a lot of scrapes before with boys his own age but had never knocked out a grown man. Standing over his fallen foe, he could hear laughter coming from the porch, most certainly directed at the victim of Isaac's punch.

Then a slurred, drunken voice called out, "—Hey, that might be that murderin' boy they lookin' fer!"

Isaac took hold of Joy's hand, and they took off running. He could hear the patter of footsteps on the gravel behind them and knew that they were being chased. Darting into an alley, they zigzagged around wooden crates and then found themselves in a shipyard. Isaac gave a furtive glance behind them and could see at least three men, possibly more, in hot pursuit.

"We have to find a place to hide, Joy!"

A row of warehouses sat silent and dark on the waterside, and the two youths instinctively headed toward them. Once among them, they desperately sought a place of concealment, but all the doors were padlocked. Rounding a corner of a small brick building, a bulky arm shot out and wrapped itself around Isaac's neck, sweeping him off his feet and pulling him into an open doorway.

"Isaac!" Joy screamed.

Joy ran after them and when she was inside, the man holding Isaac slammed the door shut and locked it. He was holding a knife against Isaac's neck, the sharp point touching his skin.

The terrified boy was grinding his teeth, expecting the blade to sweep across his neck, but the man just held it and placed a finger up to his lips, telling Joy to remain silent. Outside, they could hear the shuffling footsteps and low drunken voices of their pursuers as they passed by.

"I think they turned this corner," a subdued voice said. "They musta headed for the wharf!"

The voices drifted off, becoming indistinct and then finally muted altogether. The man pushed Isaac against the wall, ripped the duffel bag off his back, and threw it on the earthen floor, which was covered in wood chips. They were in a small warehouse of sorts. There were crates filled with block and tackle and spars lying about, along with buoys and other nautical material.

"Please, sir, let us go," Joy said.

Their captor was a large middle-aged, clean-shaven man wearing a blue sack coat and peaked cap. His narrow beady eyes seemed to disappear into his skull which was centered by a narrow, crooked nose. His square, dimpled chin jutted out like the Rock of Gibraltar.

An oil lamp sat on the table illuminating the musty room. Keeping Isaac pinned to the wall with one powerful hand, he pointed to a dusty bin next to a pair of shovels.

"You, girl! Git me thet rope in da bin and be quick or he gits it!"

She quickly brought him the rope, taking special notice of the shovels. He had pulled Isaac's cloak off and spied the cache of weapons attached to his belt. His evil eyes sparkled with delight.

"Ah! I bloody well knew it! Me luck finally catches me at the right time! 'Tis the murderin' lad the whole county is aftuh. Old Tom finally snatches a score!"

He unbuckled Isaac's belt, letting it fall to the floor. A struggle then ensued. The boy attempted to slip away, but Old Tom grabbed him in a powerful bear hug and slammed him down into a pile of wood chips. He quickly bound Isaac's wrists behind his back, then hauled him to his feet and forced him down into a chair next to the table with the lamp.

"You sit thar, boy and don't move or I'll cut yuh tuh ribbons!"

Old Tom turned to Joy, who had picked up one of the shovels and was holding it up, threatening to swing.

"You let him go!" she screamed. "He didn't murder anyone!"

Old Tom chuckled, holding out his hands in front of him and advancing slowly toward her. "Put thet shovel down befer I brain yuh wid it, girlie!"

Joy raised the shovel over her head. Surprisingly, she was not worried about what might happen to her. Her only thought was for Isaac. She was not going to let him be taken as long as she might be able to do something about it —even if she died in the attempt to free him. Her eyes met Isaac's, who motioned with his head for her to move to the right. She immediately grasped his intent.

There was a deep drop down into the lower part of the building. If she moved to the right, Old Tom would naturally follow her. She did just that and when the brute was standing on the edge, Isaac jumped out of the chair and using his shoulder, barreled into the big man's waist, causing the monster to lose his balance. Tripping, he fell off the step, landing on the lower floor hard on his right shoulder. The momentum carried Isaac over the edge, but the limber boy rolled with it and came up to his knees quickly, just in time to see Joy swing the shovel down on Old Tom's head.

She quickly untied Isaac's wrists and they checked on the would-be bounty hunter who was knocked out cold but still breathing. Isaac quickly tied him up with the rope.

"That ought to hold him until we are long gone," he said with a cheery face. Joy, too, was smiling but then her face saddened.

"What? What is it, Joy?"

She ran to him and gave the boy a hug, wrapping her thin arms around his waist.

"I...I thought you were done for," she said weakly. He felt her body go limp and caught her before she collapsed.

"Joy!"

Isaac reacted quickly. Placing her down on the floor, he used the rolled-up blanket for a pillow and threw his cloak over her. She was having one of her spells, but this one seemed worse than usual. He poured a little water on a cloth and held it on her forehead. He had seen her doing this and it seemed to help. Slowly she began to regain her senses. Her eyes were glassy but then slowly focused on Isaac's worried face.

"Oh...that was a bad one," she whispered. "I am quite dizzy, Isaac."

He was sitting next to her, holding the cloth on her forehead. "Don't worry none, Joy. We will get out of this fix. I promise we will."

She smiled and closed her eyes. "Just let me rest my eyes for a few minutes and we shall go."

"Of course, Joy. I'll sit here for as long as it takes."

He glanced up at the burning flame in the lamp. It was almost hypnotic as it danced around on the wick. For a few minutes Joy rested comfortably and then she quickly sat up as if nothing had happened. They were gathering their things when they heard a low moan coming from the subfloor where Isaac had left Old Tom, bound with rope to one of the stout support beams.

Isaac strapped his belt back on and checked his Colt before donning his cloak. He then approached Old Tom, standing on the step a safe distance away from him. There was a stream of caked blood on the left side of the old man's face and when he saw Isaac, his countenance changed from one of subdued resignation to fear. The smirking boy was holding the Colt in his left hand and Old Tom's gaze was squarely focused on it.

"Now, watcha gonna do, lad? Don't do nuthin foolish now, yuh hear?"

"Why not?" Isaac said calmly. "I'm just about tired of mean people. I've taken care of a few of you scoundrels in the last couple of days and if I must, I'll dispose of a few more. I'm taking this girl to the Freedom Road, and no one is going to stop me. You see, I have right on my side. God's looking out for me and this girl and people like you are powerless to do anything about it. You can tell that to whoever you want..."

Joy was beside him. "Come on, Isaac. It's getting late."

They walked out into the darkness. Next stop, the African church.

Or so they hoped.

Chapter 14

Isaac's left hand was throbbing. He had almost forgotten he had used it on that docker's chin. He didn't tell Joy, as she would fuss over it and would want to fix it up. That might delay their arrival at the African church, and they needed to get there. The sooner they did, the sooner they would be out of harm's way. Wil Jericho was somewhere within the town, or possibly in Norfolk. He would be casing the wharfs and shipyards, reasoning that the fugitives would attempt to stow away on a vessel bound for the sea. Elijah would, by now, have gotten that message through to Major Frost.

At least he hoped he had managed to send it.

They crept along the wharves, attempting to keep to the shadows as much as possible. Joy attempted to gather her bearings, but nothing looked familiar to her. They had gotten lost after they had fled from the dockers. They crossed into an intersection of two roads.

"North Street!" she exclaimed. "We only have to follow this road and we shall find it."

Isaac let Joy lead the way. It was nearing the witching hour and fortunately the streets were deserted. They passed by another tavern and could hear somebody banging on a piano along with raucous laughter. Luckily no one noticed them. They arrived at the church a few minutes later. It was dark and foreboding. Not a light to be seen shined through any of the stain glass windows.

"This place looks deserted," Isaac said.

"Let's try the front door."

Isaac knocked and then tried turning the knob, but it wouldn't budge. "It is locked. Maybe there is a side entrance?"

They started to turn around when they perceived a slight mechanical sound as if a bolt were turning in a lock. The door cracked open, and a wizened old head popped out from the darkness. A woman, well on in years, stood in the doorway holding a candle, the flame revealing her long, gray, scraggly locks and wrinkled face. In fact, the face was so grotesque with its beak-shaped nose and moles, it startled Joy, who instinctively stepped back and grasped Isaac's arm for protection.

For a few seconds the old woman merely held the candle up in front of her, attempting to get a better look at the two youths standing out in the cold night. She then motioned with her withered and spotted hand to enter. They followed her into the church and immediately detected a smell as if the walls had recently been painted. She shut the door behind them and turned the latch, locking it. She then pointed to a pew.

"Sit. I shall return shortly," she said in a gruff voice. She set off at a brisk pace in a manner befitting someone much younger. They observed her opening another door through which she disappeared, leaving them sitting alone in the darkness.

Joy tapped Isaac on the arm. "She looks like a witch." There was a hint of a smile on her cherubic face.

He whispered into her ear jokingly, "She might cast a spell on us!"

They both giggled, being careful to keep their laughter soft.

"I feel terrible walking into a house of God with all these weapons," Isaac said quietly.

Joy placed her soft hand on top of his.

"I think God would understand, Isaac."

"I hope so."

The side door opened, and the old lady emerged, this time holding a lantern.

"Come," she said, beckoning them with her hand. "Follow me. You cannot stay here. It is too dangerous for you."

They followed her outside and across the street into an alley where there were some rough-looking tenement houses, each one a patchwork of boards and mismatched pieces of lumber. The roofs were built, for the most part, from whatever material their occupants might find. They entered a small courtyard almost devoid of grass, where a few unhealthy-looking chickens scurried about after detecting their approach. The buildings here were even more wretched-looking than the ones they had passed on their way to town. To one of these small shanties the old woman led them. Inside, the dirt floor was strewn with hay and rusty farm tools.

The old woman held the lantern up in front of their faces. She stood only inches away. Isaac could smell her rancid breath and did his best not to show the disgust on his face. Joy, too, was having issues with it. She wanted to vomit.

"I am Ada. And you must be Isaac and Joy," she said with a hint of a northern accent.

Isaac was stunned. "You knew we were coming?"

"Not exactly, but you are the news of the town. When you showed up at the church, I guessed immediately who you were. After all, how many little white boys and little Black girls would be traveling together in the middle of the night?"

Isaac and Joy glanced at each other and smiled.

"So you can help us?" Isaac asked. "I need to get a message to Major Frost at Fort Norfolk. He is my friend and can help us. He is the one who gave me the address of the church, should I need it. I am most fortunate he did so."

The old woman looked forlorn. The large, hairy mole on the bridge of her nose seemed to glow in the light of the lantern.

"Indeed, he might be able to help. I shall send a runner over on a barge to him in the morning, but I must say there is probably little that he can do unless he can stash you on an outgoing vessel. Your case is a civil matter, and the military has no jurisdiction."

"But he must help us. It is our only hope!" Isaac pleaded.

"I must tell you this," the old woman said. "A Mr. Jericho came calling just before dark. He has reason to believe you might seek assistance from

our church. I do believe he knows Joy here has
visited the place with Mrs. Jericho. He is coming
back in the morning. That is why I have brought
you here. The church is no sanctuary for you at the
present. Now, before I leave, there is something I
must show you."

They followed her to a dusty coal bin set up
against an otherwise empty wall in the shack.
Handing the lantern to Isaac, she lifted the lid.

"What do you see?" she asked, picking up a
piece of coal and rubbing it between two
attenuated fingers.

Isaac was confused. "Coal?"

"Indeed, that is what you are supposed to
see. Now look here."

She pointed to a crack on the side of the bin
that worked its way around to the front. "What do
you see there?"

Isaac shrugged. "An old rusty crack in the
metal."

Ada gave them a wizened smile, showing a
mouth devoid of teeth. "Indeed, you do!"

She grabbed a crowbar and wedged it into
the crack and used it as a lever. The bin opened at
the crack and Isaac held the lantern up to the

opening that presented itself to them. He was shocked at what he saw. An opening large enough for a man to slide in led to a stairway that descended as far as the eye could see.

"Where...where does it go?" Isaac asked.

Joy stuck her head into the opening and her mouth dropped. "I...I know what this is. I have heard of it," she exclaimed excitedly. "It is the Underground Railroad! Esther told me about it, but I didn't believe her."

Isaac was puzzled. "The Underground Railroad?"

"Joy is right. However, it's not really a railroad as the term implies," Ada said. "Trains are sometimes used, but so are wagons, steamships, and the good old healthy mode of walking. There are many routes with safehouses along the way for runaway slaves and their families."

"Where does this lead?" Joy asked.

Ada pointed to the opening. "At the bottom of the stairway is a small room. It is here where you will spend the night. Someone will return for you in the morning. They will bring you food. Have you any water?"

"Yes, ma'am, nearly a full canteen," Isaac responded.

"That will get you through the night. There is plenty of dry straw to make a bed. We just changed it this morning. Keep the lantern. You will need it to keep away the rats."

Joy looked horrified.

"I...I don't like rats," she said.

"Try not to think about them," Ada replied. "One more thing: There is a small, narrow tunnel accessible from a grate in the floor. It drops only about three feet deep but runs under the ground about three-hundred feet to another grate at a secluded spot in the reeds along the riverbank. Sometimes, when the river rises, it floods, but it has been many years and you will find it dry, should you need it. But let me emphasize this: Only use it if it is absolutely necessary."

Isaac stood up. "What time will they come get us?"

"Early, perhaps just after first light, but you will not know it down in that cellar, unless you have a timepiece."

"I do," Isaac said proudly.

"Good. Now climb down and try to get some rest. As I said, I will send a runner to Fort Norfolk just before dawn. You should know something by mid-morning."

They crawled through the opening and started down the narrow wooden steps which led to a small platform. The stairs then turned to the right, and they found themselves in the room Ada had mentioned. It was cold, with the musty smell of a basement. Isaac held the lantern aloft, checking every corner of the room. A fat water rat scurried across the floor and disappeared into a hole in the wall causing Joy to shriek and clutch onto Isaac's arm. They looked at each other and burst out laughing.

"Well, I suppose we had better make the best of it," Isaac said, holding the lantern over the iron grate in the floor. There were rat droppings everywhere, but the straw looked clean, and they were thankful for that.

"Isaac, what if the lantern goes out?"

He shrugged. "I got matches and a candle but with all this straw and dry timber I would hate to use it. One mistake and this place would be a blazing inferno in no time at all." He changed the subject. "You still got some food in that bag of yours? I'm famished."

They sat down next to each other on the straw. Joy sifted through her small bag and pulled out two biscuits while he removed his belt and holsters.

"These are the last biscuits and there are only a few slabs of dried bacon left. It looks like a lean meal tonight, Isaac."

She handed him a biscuit and he said a quick prayer before he tore into it.

"I still have the apples, but the beef jerky is gone," he said with a mouthful of powdery biscuit. "Hopefully, they will bring us a good meal come morning. I have money, but if we showed ourselves at any of these grocer shops, we would almost certainly be recognized. Let's pray Major Frost can help us."

Joy took a few bites of biscuit and offered the rest of it to Isaac who reluctantly but greedily devoured it. She had lost her appetite and Isaac worried she was not eating enough. The boy then reached into his duffel bag and brought out a harmonica.

"You can play?" Joy asked.

He cocked his head to the side and winked at her. "A little. You want me to play?"

She became animated and clapped her gloved hands together. "Oh yes! Please do!"

He started out playing a soft ballad but then gradually worked up to a cheery song. He stood up and motioned for her to do the same as he started blowing the upbeat song, "Simple Gifts." Locked arm in arm, they twirled around in circles and Joy began making up words to the song. This went on for nearly ten minutes until, quite exhausted with laughter and merriment, they collapsed in the straw.

"Where did you learn that song, Isaac? That was wonderful!"

He removed his brogans and kicked back on the straw, twirling a piece of it between his fingers. "My mum was a Shaker. Sometimes, she would take me to one of the dances and I learned to play. I never really believed in all that nonsense that some of the elders preached but I enjoyed the music."

She was sitting cross-legged next to him. Her face cheery. "When we get to Massachusetts, I will play the piano for you," she said, using her fingers to simulate tapping on the keys.

He turned to his side, resting his head on his hand, gazing at her with admiration. "Really? You can play? That is grand! We can play together and even sing!"

Sitting up he clapped his hands and then winced. She immediately noticed his discomfort as he grimaced.

"Let me see your hand, Isaac."

He rolled his eyes and reluctantly held it out for her to inspect. The knuckles were chafed and one of them was swollen.

"That docker's chin was hard as a rock, but I sure gave him a wallop he won't soon forget," he said.

She reached into her bag, pulled out a small tin and opened it. He watched her dip a small cloth into the tin and gently daub the sticky substance on his knuckles.

"Is that honey?" he asked.

"It is. I find that it works wonders in the healing process," she responded. She tied the cloth around his hand and then raised it to her lips and kissed it "There. You'll feel better in no time," she said, with a wide grin.

He was staring at her with admiration. "I feel better already, Joy."

They sat musing and watched as another rat poked its head through the grate, whiskers twitching, before thinking better of its new surroundings and disappearing back into the tunnel. The cellar was cold, but Joy wrapped the blanket around their shoulders and coupled with the straw, they were warm enough to pass the night in relative comfort.

****

Isaac awoke with a start. For a few seconds, he lay there listening. Something had awakened him. He heard it again. A dull thumping sound from up above.

The first thing he noticed was that the lantern had gone out. He could hear Joy's shallow breathing next to him and he decided not to wake her. It might be nothing but his imagination running wild. He felt for his belt and pistols. They were still next to him. He told himself to calm down, but when the thumping sound was heard again, his heart began to race. This time it was much louder, and it awakened Joy. She instinctively tapped Isaac on the shoulder, not being able to see him in the darkness.

"Isaac, what was that?"

"I don't know."

She nudged closer to him and heard him cocking one of his pistols. "It might be Ada or one of the other conductors," she said.

"I wish that lantern had not gone out," Isaac whispered.

"Well, that might be for the best right now," she said. "If someone does happen to find this room, they won't think there would be anyone down here in the darkness."

Isaac agreed but fumbled around in his duffel bag searching for his tin. He finally found it and struck a match, holding it over the lantern.

"There is still oil," he said. He then looked at his pocket watch.

"It is half past six. We have been sleeping for hours," he said, blowing out the match.

Another loud thump caused them to jump. Isaac clutched the Colt tighter. Suddenly, a grating noise and a soft light appeared at the curve of the stairway. They held their breath and waited.

Chapter 15

For a few seconds it was quiet. The only sound came from their shallow breathing. A dim light from the stairway seemed to suggest somebody had opened the secret passage and was holding a lantern in the opening. Suddenly, there was the sound of movement, of footsteps descending, and the light became brighter, revealing a single boot followed by another one settling on the platform. Whoever they belonged to obviously needed a rest as they did not move for a few seconds. When they finally did, a large stick moved with them, assisting a pair of bowlegs down the final few steps.

The youths relaxed. The old man standing at the bottom of the stairway holding a lantern and a heavy oak cane was no threat to them. He appeared to be as old—or even older than Ada, if that was even possible. His white locks hung down around his temples, but the top of his head had long ago given up sprouting any hair follicles, except for a few stringy gray strands, like weeds sprouting out of an untended garden. Isaac lowered his Colt and, stuffing it back in his holster, stood up and strapped his belt back on.

"Muh name's Hubert. Wasn't sure yuh was still hidin' down here," the old man said in an ancient, gravelly voice. "Didn't see no light. Miss Ada sez yuh had a light."

"The light went out sometime during the night," Joy said.

The old man was breathing heavy. It was obvious making the trek down the stairs had taken the wind out of his sails. He slung a pack from his shoulders and set it down in front of Isaac, who was in the process of lacing up his brogans.

"Food from Miss Ada. But yuh gotsta run. The posse goin' house tuh house lookin' fer yuh both. Word on the street is they gonna make people talk. A bad man leadin' 'em. Jericho's his name and he got the sheriff lookin', too."

Isaac swallowed nervously, quickly stuffing the satchel of food into his duffel bag. "But where can we go? Can we not stay here?" he asked the old man, with desperation.

Hubert shook his head, his sad eyes feeling their despair. "They holdin' two of our conductors' feet tuh the fire. One of 'em is bound tuh crack. Yuh gotsta go. Not sho' who yuh are boy, or you neither, girl, but I ain't evuh seen 'em crackin' the whip like this afore."

Isaac was desperate. "Sir, did Miss Ada get word to Major Frost for us?"

Hubert shrugged. "Don't know nuthin about that."

A banging from up above told them someone was up there. Hubert's head shot around toward the stairway. His milky white, cataract-filled eyes showed fear. "Yuh need tuh go now!"

Thinking quickly, Isaac struck a match and lit the lantern. They gathered their things while old Hubert stood looking down at the iron grate in the floor.

"Ah don't have the strength in these old hands like I had in the days of muh youth. Yuh gonna have tuh lift the iron, young boy."

Isaac reached down and yanked on the lid and felt it budge. With some effort, he managed to move it, sliding it across the floor enough to where they could fit into the hole.

"What about you? If they find you here, they will certainly kill you," Isaac said. "Can you come with us?"

"No," the old man said. "I could never crawl through that tunnel. My bones are brittle and muh days are numbered anyhow. I'll take what fate gives me, young'uns. Go now! Afore it is too late!"

Taking the lead, Isaac dropped his duffel bag down into the hole and quickly lowered himself down. Joy handed him the lantern and he helped her down. He looked up and could see Hubert standing above, anxiously peering down at them.

"I hear voices! Quick, go!"

Isaac held the lantern out in front of him. He was chewing on his lip and could feel Joy clutching the sleeve of his cloak.

"I...I don't like this, Isaac."

The tunnel was about three feet high and about the same width. It was lined with old kiln bricks, and he wondered how long it had been in use. It smelled like rotten eggs. The lantern only cast its light for about twenty feet before the glow was absorbed by the pitch darkness.

They started to crawl along. Isaac felt claustrophobic, as if the weight of the world was pinning him to the ground. He stopped and closed his eyes. He did not like confined spaces.

"What's wrong?" Joy asked, tugging on one of his ankles.

"I...I need to stop for a second, that's all," he said, trying not to show fear. He opened his eyes and started again. They had crawled about a hundred feet when they heard a loud crack as if a gun had been fired.

Isaac froze, turning and holding the lantern behind him. He could see shock and bewilderment on Joy's face. Neither one of them had to say anything to know what probably had just happened. Poor Hubert had met his maker.

First Moses and now Hubert. Isaac wondered how many more would sacrifice themselves. Without uttering a sound, they continued along the narrow passage until Isaac spotted something ahead of him. It was a dark lump that seemed to be growing out of the bricks.

"There is an obstacle ahead of us," he said nervously.

Joy crammed her thin body up alongside his to get a better look. "What is that thing?"

Isaac pulled his Bowie knife out of his makeshift sheath. "Might be some kind of animal. Stay behind me."

He placed the blade's handle between his teeth and started forward. As he inched nearer the lump, it began to take shape. The first thing he noticed was a dried leather boot, and then, with horror, he realized what it was in front of them— a human body. He felt a lump in his throat.

The corpse had obviously been there for a long time. It had undergone the process of desiccation. The wrinkled skin was taut against the muted skull, the long, dark hair hanging around the temples in unruly patches. It was an appalling spectacle and Isaac turned his head away in disgust. He felt like retching. "It's a man's body," he said with disgust, turning around and facing Joy.

"Well, it surely cannot harm us," she said. "I have seen plenty of dead bodies before."

He swallowed and she noticed his eyes widen with terror. "Joy, behind us," he whispered. His voice was filled with dread.

She turned, seeing that a dim light had appeared. Someone else had entered the tunnel!

"We need to hurry!" Isaac exclaimed.

They brushed by the mummified body, which was on its side with one of its arms extended forward, the bony index finger pointing toward the exit of the tunnel as if it were telling them to get a move on.

They picked up the pace. Isaac knew whoever was following them was likely at a disadvantage, being bigger than the youths.

The tunnel seemed to drag on endlessly until they finally and mercifully reached the end. A heavy iron grate blocked the exit which was also covered with dead reeds from the riverbank and small sticks that had fallen through the slats. Isaac gave the lantern to Joy and attempted to push the grate with his hands but found that it wouldn't budge.

"Let me help," Joy whispered.

Together, they pushed with all their strength, but still, the iron held fast. That is when they heard the voice calling from behind them, a distant echo that sounded distorted by the narrow tunnel but unmistakably issuing from the maniacal throat of Wil Jericho.

"Cousin Isaac, the doors are closing shut, boy! Ah'm comin' fer yuh!"

Isaac was desperate and decided to try something. He got on his back and with a swift kick at the grate felt it budge.

"It moved!" Joy exclaimed.

He kicked again and this time the grate came loose, toppled over through the reeds, sliding part way down the embankment, the wet grass acting like a slide. Isaac poked his head out into the darkness and felt the cool wind and a gentle mist on his face. It was still dark, and a dense fog hung over the river like a comforting blanket. "It's a good cover, Joy. This fog is as thick as pea soup!"

He took the lantern from her and suddenly an idea came to him. There were dead falls lying about on the bank, and gathering an armload he threw them into the tunnel's entrance. Joy knew exactly what he was up to and assisted him with packing the hole with fuel. When they were done, Isaac took the lantern and threw it into the tunnel. They stood back for a few seconds and watched the inferno. The entrance of the tunnel soon resembled a gateway to hell.

"The smoke alone will force them to go back," Isaac reasoned.

He took Joy's hand, and they scrambled down the embankment, disappearing into the shrouded mist until they found themselves on a level shore.

"Which way?" Joy asked.

Isaac had not even bothered to think about it. He had been so busy worrying about getting out of the tunnel, he had not thought about their next move. Since they no longer had a safehouse, his only thought was to somehow cross the river and attempt to gain Fort Norfolk. But how?

He conferred with Joy, and they agreed that it was their best chance, but first they would need to find a secure place to hide. The fog would provide cover for them, but it wouldn't be long before Wil Jericho and his minions found the tunnel's exit, and then the search would begin along the shoreline in earnest, especially when the fog lifted.

Somewhere in the river, a foghorn sounded, and Isaac thought about Captain Mayberry and the *Pegasus*. If they could only get across the river, their troubles would be lessened somewhat.

They headed along the rocky shoreline and stumbled upon a narrow trail that led up the embankment. Isaac decided to follow it to see where it led them. He was out of options. They needed to find a place of refuge, and quickly, before daylight and the lifting of the fog. With any luck, word would have gotten to Major Frost, and he would be looking for them. He thought about Elijah. He, too, would be attempting to help them in any way he could manage.

Stumbling up the path, they found it led to a foot bridge that crossed some marshland. For a minute they stood there trying to decide whether to cross it. The fog was so thick, they could not see the other side. Joy was about to suggest they try it when she happened to glance over the railing and see the bow of a small rowboat. "Isaac, look!"

Carefully, they descended through the reeds. They could see the boat was lashed to one of the posts.

"Do you think that we can row this across the river?" she asked Isaac.

The boy had done a lot of rowing on Bandy's pond, but this here was different. The Elizabeth River was subject to tidal currents and was at least a half a mile across, maybe more. Also, there was the danger of being rammed by a steamer or other large vessel in the fog, not to mention the risk of merely capsizing from an errant wave.

He weighed their options. How else would they be able get across? They could stow away on a barge or perhaps a steamer, but that, too, came with risks. If they were caught, they would be trapped. He would be arrested and remanded over to the sheriff. Joy would be returned to Jericho Plantation. All would be lost.

"I wonder if this thing is seaworthy?" Isaac said, climbing into the small boat.

He checked it for leaks. It was obviously a crabber's boat. There was a net, along with a floatable cork jacket and a few rusty tin cans under the rear seat. Painted across the stern in white paint was the name, *Water Wizard*.

"Well, Joy, let's give it a try. I don't see where we have much choice. If we wait until daylight, this place might be swarming with rascals looking for us. Can you swim?"

She was already in the boat, placing the oars in the locks, a look of fierce resilience on her face. "No, I cannot swim. But we must try this, Isaac. Let us put faith in the Lord who thus far has been watching over us."

Isaac removed his shoes and stockings, rolled up his pant legs to the knees, and waded out into the salt marsh. The water was cold. He untied the rope from the post used as the boats mooring mast. He then reached into his coat and pulled out a few silver dollars and bank notes and tied them in a silk handkerchief which he attached to the hanging rope.

"Whoever this craft belongs to will be able to buy another outfit," he said.

He then pushed the boat until it had been dislodged from the bank and leaped in. He helped Joy into the cumbersome cork vest before taking his seat at the oars. It wasn't long before Isaac had weaved the boat through the marsh into the river.

"How can you navigate in this fog?" Joy asked. "We might be going around in circles."

He smiled. "The river flows in one direction. As long as it is always the same on the port side of the boat, we will be traveling true, though the current may take us farther along than we want. The last thing we need is to be pulled out into Chesapeake Bay."

Joy was sitting on the bow, peering out into the dense mist. "I sure wish we hadn't destroyed that lantern," she said. "We could use it about now. I can't see more than a few feet in any direction."

Though they couldn't see the sun, they perceived the sky lightening in the east through the murky haze. It would be daylight soon. They hoped to be across the river by the time the fog lifted. Isaac felt his arms tiring as he struggled against the current. Occasionally, he would stop for a few seconds to rest, but the boat would drift, and it always seemed to want to go back toward the Portsmouth shore. He plodded along and Joy decided to raise his spirits by humming "Go Tell it on the Mountain."

Isaac broke out into a smile and joined her. Soon, they were singing it as loud as their young voices would carry. They had just finished a stanza when they perceived a low humming sound, and the thick haze began to lighten off the starboard side of their small craft. With horror, Isaac realized what it was: a steamer.

And it was bearing down right at them.

Chapter 16

The sound of the foghorn was deafening as the paddle steamer bore down on the *Water Wizard*. Isaac and Joy were frantically attempting to figure out which way they needed to row. It was finally agreed that the larger vessel was bearing down somewhat aft of them. Isaac decided that to continue forward was the prudent course of action.

Isaac's muscles were on fire, the paddles striking into the foamy water with an intensity that could only be brought about by desperation and survival instinct.

Finally, out of the mist appeared the massive bow of the steamer. The bright light cutting the fog in two. It was like a ghost ship, the waves breaking from both sides of it. It was a surreal spectacle, and Isaac and Joy both knew it was over for them. A giant wave cast the *Water Wizard* aloft and for a few seconds they believed they were airborne. However, the small vessel had merely ridden the high crest of the wave before it came crashing down in the trough. Somehow, miraculously, Isaac had managed to stay in the boat, but Joy had lost her grip and tumbled into the cold water.

"Joy!" Isaac screamed as the stern of the steamer disappeared into the mist, the sound of its chugging engine swallowing up the boy's desperate voice.

He scanned the water around the boat in all directions but could see nothing in the fog. His eyes filled with tears as he perched precariously on the bow of the *Water Wizard* where Joy had been sitting just a few short minutes before.

"Joy! Please answer me," he cried. The tears flowing down his healthy red cheeks. He began to sob uncontrollably. Then he heard a faint cry out of the fog.

"Isaac! Isaac!"

His head whipped around in the direction of the voice, eyes darting from side to side. The fog was breaking up and patches of the dark, choppy river were becoming visible. The foghorn from the ship that had almost rammed them blew into the misty morning, sounding distant, and that is when Isaac saw it—a small head bobbing up and down with the frothy water.

He reacted swiftly. Discarding his cloak, coat, shirt, cap, and belt, he gathered a long rope that he found under the bench seat among the nets. He quickly tied a figure eight around the cleat and the other end tightly around his waist and, without any further consideration for his own safety, dived into the chilly water. Although the water was cold, it was not freezing. He was an expert swimmer and reached Joy within a minute.

"Isaac," she whispered, as he threw her thin arm around his shoulder. He treaded water with his free arm, using his legs like fins. Finally, and with great effort, he reached the boat. With some difficulty, he managed to pull himself up, almost capsizing the boat, and then reached over and lifted Joy out of the water.

They were both shivering but he removed her cork jacket and wet shawl and wrapped her in his warm coat and cloak, leaving him with only his cotton shirt, wet breeches, and cap to protect him from the elements. He then gathered his bearings and set to work with the oars. They had to find warmth and find it soon or risk perishing from hypothermia.

He rowed like a galley slave into the patchy fog, his teeth chattering, his wet, flaxen hair plastered over his face. Joy sat on the small bench seat, huddled in Isaac's cloak. She was shivering miserably. He was astonished, however, when she suddenly leaned forward and attempted to grab the oars.

"Joy, what are you doing?"

She tried to smile, her round face glowing. She was shaking with the cold, letting the cloak fall from her thin shoulders.

"L—Let me row for a while. You're tired."

He stopped rowing and threw the cloak back over her shoulders. "No, you can barely sit there, never mind row. We are almost to the other side. I can feel it."

She knew he was right. Her body temperature had dropped, and she was slowly drifting off. Isaac could sense her slipping away and his exertions at the oars became more intense, even superhuman. He had no idea where his strength was coming from.

Finally, he detected a faint noise in front of them and his spirits soared. It was the sound of waves lapping up on the shore. A minute later he could see a rocky beach and headed for it. A loud grating sound told him that the *Water Wizard* had struck bottom. He leaped into the shallow water, knee-deep, and pulled the boat up onto the shore, lashing it to a small sapling. He had no idea where they were, only that they had landed somewhere on the Norfolk side of the river in a wooded forest.

Joy climbed out of the boat, staggered up the rocky beach, and collapsed under a pine tree.

"Joy, this is providence. We have landed in a forest. Let us find some place where we can make a fire before we perish from the cold."

She tried to rise but her legs would not work. He squatted down in front of her.

"Wrap your arms around my shoulders," he said.

She did so and he lifted her on his back. Despite her light frame, Isaac struggled with her weight. He was exhausted and how he managed to carry her, he did not know, but he did not complain. Joy, too, was selfless. She was not thinking about herself, only him. She looked down.

"Isaac, where are your shoes?"

He wrinkled his nose. "They went in the drink when the boat almost capsized and threw you into the water. We lost everything, Joy. My duffel bag and your satchel and blanket are out there in the river somewhere, but I still have my weapons. I also have my tin of matches in the cloak you are wearing. I'll have a fire blazing in no time, you'll see."

She playfully pulled on his ear. "We haven't lost everything, Isaac."

He smiled. "We were lucky to make it across with our lives. I thought we were done for, Joy."

Isaac finally found what he was looking for— a quiet spot, far away from any foot traffic in what appeared to be a gutted-out ancient cellar of a house. He set Joy down and gathered some wood. Within a few minutes, he had a fire blazing and set Joy's wet shawl up on a nearby tree branch to dry. He took inventory of their stock. Luckily, he had kept most of his money in his cloak and he also had the small sum that was stitched inside his cap. He had a loaded derringer, his Colt and Bowie knife, but the rest of his spare bullets and powder had ended up in the river, as did the food that Hubert had given them.

"We will need to find food and water," he said, adding a stick to the flames.

The warmth from the fire had revitalized Joy somewhat. She was able to stand up and fished inside the pocket of her drying cloak.

"I saved you a slab of bacon," she said, throwing him the dried meat. "It is the last piece, but you need to eat it. I know you are famished from all that rowing, so don't try and give it back to me. If I must, I'll come over there and force you to eat it."

He rubbed the bacon between his dirty fingers, staring at it as if it were the last piece on Earth. She was watching him carefully, a pleasant smile on her face.

"Okay, I tried to warn you," she said, shuffling over to him with a mischievous smirk on her glowing face. Sitting down next to him she took his hand and brought it up to his lips. He felt his mouth watering but at the same time, something else stirred within him.

"Close your eyes and open your mouth," she said. "Doctor's orders."

He chuckled, playing along, and he did as she bid. She stuffed the bacon in his mouth. He chewed on it, mechanically. She sat there giggling.

"Can I open my eyes?" he asked, when he had finished swallowing his meager fare.

"Yup. Doctor's orders."

He opened them and blinked in an exaggerated way as if he had been blind and just regained his sight. They both burst out laughing and then, when they were done with their childish amusement, their faces became serious, and he did something quite unexpectant. He leaned over and kissed her on the cheek. It was an impulsive thing to do, but quite natural. She felt herself blushing.

"Did you just kiss me?" she asked.

He nodded. "I...I couldn't help myself, Joy," he said nervously. "I...I've never done that before. I'm sorry."

She shrugged. "Well, if you're sorry, I am, too, because I can't help myself either." She leaned over and kissed him on the cheek.

He smiled, showing her his white teeth, and then gazed dreamily into the fire. "I...I have never had a real friend before, Joy. Besides Bandy, I mean. Have you?"

She shot him a look of tenderness, her doe-like brown eyes blinking rapidly. "No...well...my sister, but you know... She is my sister. She's not like you."

He chuckled and added a stick to the flames. "Yeah...definitely not like me."

She giggled, removing Isaac's cloak, and wrapping it around both of their shoulders. They huddled together in front of the fire, feeling its warmth. Despite their predicament, they briefly found themselves without a care in the world.

Isaac took stock of their situation. Despite losing his duffel bag and shoes, they were still in a better situation than they had been only a few hours before. They had managed to cross the river.

He had no idea where Fort Norfolk was located, or, for that matter, where they had landed. He assumed they must be close to Norfolk, possibly near the fort. They would rest and let their clothes dry and then attempt to find out exactly where they were.

Joy began to massage her temples, and he knew that she was having one of her spells. He made a bed of pine boughs and wrapped her in his cloak, next to the fire, and she was soon asleep. He wanted to stay awake. After all, they had slept for a few hours in the safehouse, but since that time his exertions had taxed him to his physical limits. He felt sleepy.

Gathering some more wood for the fire, he sat down with his back against a large loblolly pine a dozen feet or so from the fire. He removed his Colt from the holster and set it down in his lap. If anyone entered his camp and tried anything, he would be ready. He felt his eyelids drooping and as much as he tried to fight it, sleep finally overtook him.

He awoke with a start. The first thing he noticed was that the sun was high in the sky and the fog had lifted. In fact, it was a sunny day and pleasantly warm. He rubbed his eyes and when they began to clear, they focused on the fire which was still blazing. Had Joy added wood?

She was still sleeping, wrapped in his cloak. Confused, he stood up and that is when he saw the man sitting on the opposite side of the fire, partially hidden by the smoke. His heart began to race. He reached for his Colt, but it was gone. His derringer, too, had been removed from its holster which left him with the Bowie knife. He quickly pulled Joy away from the threat. She awoke with confusion but when she saw the man sitting a few feet away, she immediately latched onto Isaac's arm.

Isaac held the Bowie knife in front of him and waved it toward the man.

"Who...who are you?" Isaac asked. "What are you doing in our camp?"

The man was sitting cross-legged holding his hands up to the flames. Isaac could see his pale, clean-shaven face. He was rather young, wearing black, with a mop of curly brown hair and jutting chin. He looked up at them and held out his hands as if to show him that he was unarmed and no threat to them. That is when Isaac smelled the bacon sizzling on a skillet over the fire, along with a pot of boiling coffee.

"I apologize for taking your pistols as you slept," the stranger said in a low but firm voice, "but I feared you might react hastily and send me to my great reward had you woken suddenly. They are here next to me, and you can have them back if you would like."

Cautiously, Isaac approached the man and, like a dog fearing a trick, he quickly snatched his pistols up and stuffed them back in the holsters on his belt, never taking his eyes off the stranger. That is when he noticed the white collar.

"You're a priest?"

The stranger nodded. "I am John Brooke, the vicar of St. Christopher's parish. Do you know who St. Christopher was?"

Isaac looked at Joy and together they shook their heads.

"He is the patron saint of travelers. How ironic, yes? But have a seat and join me for breakfast."

Isaac and Joy relaxed.

"Father, forgive me for holding my knife against you in a threatening manner," Isaac said. "Had I known you were a priest I never would have done so. But the young girl here—her name is Joy—is under my protection, and I am going to get her to Massachusetts where she will be free. My name is—"

The priest interrupted him. "There is no need for you to tell me, young knight. I know it."

"You do?"

"It is Isaac Barker. You are quite famous, as is Joy."

The girl glanced at Isaac whose eyes had narrowed in contemplative reverie.

"Are...are you going to turn us in to the sheriff?" Joy asked.

"Of course not, Joy," the priest responded. "The duty of St. Christopher is to assist the weary traveler on his or her journey. Right is might and you, Isaac and Joy, are God's children traveling down the path of righteousness. Now, sit by the fire and join me for the wonderful breakfast God has provided us, and you can tell me all about your journey. This morning's newspaper is full of cunning lies."

They sat down next to the priest who turned the bacon with a large fork. The grease spilling into the fire sizzled. Isaac heard his empty stomach growling and couldn't wait to dig his teeth into the savory meat.

He related to the priest all that had happened to him over the previous few weeks. Joy then told her story about how Isaac had arrived and become her protector. The priest listened to their stories with a keen interest and when they were done, he removed the crispy bacon from the skillet and placed it on a clean tin plate. He then reached into his satchel and pulled out a half dozen hardboiled eggs. Isaac's eyes widened with delight. Impulsively, he reached for one and the priest stopped him by gently touching his hand.

"We thank God and all he has provided us first."

"Oh, yes, Father. I apologize for my bad manners, sir."

"No need," the good priest responded. He said grace and mumbled a prayer in Latin, which the two youths attempted to follow with bowed heads. When he was done, he crossed himself as did Isaac and Joy and, like magic, two more tin plates suddenly appeared.

The food was then divided up into three equal portions by the priest. Isaac's stomach seemed to growl with displeasure at the delay but with patience, he finally received his reward. The boy stuffed a whole egg into his mouth and the chewing process began in earnest. Joy, much more dignified, took small bites, and by the time Isaac had swallowed two eggs and a slab of bacon, she was barely finished with half an egg.

The priest produced three stone mugs from his satchel and poured each of them a hot coffee. Isaac closed his eyes and took a sip, feeling its immediate soothing effects.

"Father, how did you know we were here?" Isaac asked.

"I was taking my morning stroll along the riverbank and happened to stumble upon a boat. It had not been there the day before. I also discerned by the small footprints along the beach that they might belong to children and, furthermore, suspected they might belong to the two fugitives I had heard about the evening before. So, curious, I set off to see what I could find and, behold, I found your camp and the two of you slumbering. Not wishing to disturb you, I returned to the church kitchen and brought the breakfast we are now enjoying."

Joy swallowed a mouthful of coffee. "What are they saying about us in the city?"

"The newspaper printed a description of you along with the purported crime of murder. Young Isaac here has a hundred-dollar bounty on his head, and you, Joy, are to be returned to your master if captured, apparently without any other consequences. Although, a few of the people I have talked to on the streets seem to be ambivalent as to why this supposed murder occurred. There are some who find it hard to believe a boy Isaac's age could commit such a heinous crime without some justification."

Joy was tapping the rim of her mug with her small thumb, her large brown eyes looking at Isaac with admiration.

"Well," she said quietly, "we have told you the truth of the matter and Isaac is no murderer. But how do we convince people he is not?"

The priest placed a comforting hand on Joy's shoulder. He was wearing a solemn expression.

"That, young lady, is going to be the tricky part. We live in a vengeful, hateful society. If you had been a white girl and Isaac had rescued you from an attacker, he would be regarded a hero. Because you are a slave and Black, there is a different narrative. It is hypocrisy at its finest."

The priest emphasized his point by holding up a finger and wagging it back and forth as if he were delivering a homily.

Isaac was standing up, holding his mug of coffee in both hands, his face pensive and determined. "Father Brooke, we need to get to Fort Norfolk. Can you help us, sir?"

The priest smiled. "I will do all I can do to help you. However, once word gets around that you might have crossed the river, there will be bounty hunters and other lawmen swarming these woods in search of you. You must come with me to the church. You will be safe there until I can get word to Fort Norfolk."

They finished their coffee and Father Brooke helped Isaac extinguish the fire. Isaac and Joy were surprised how close they had camped to the church. It was just over a small hill, on the edge of the city. The priest informed them that Fort Norfolk was not far away, and he would immediately set out to give Major Frost, Isaac's message. Of course, there was always the chance the good major was already out looking for his friend.

The church was a small one, but expertly built with stone. It reminded Isaac of some of the large cathedrals he had seen sketches of in his father's old books. The stained-glass windows were also impressive. Father Brooke told them they had come from an ancient edifice in the Black Country of England and were hundreds of years old. Isaac felt himself drawn to one of them. It was a pastoral scene that showed a wizened old shepherd and his flock of sheep. The white-bearded shepherd seemed to be gazing up at a beacon of light in the sky. Isaac pointed it out to Joy and the priest.

"This is remarkable," Isaac said. "Look at how the sun shines directly on that window at this very moment!"

"God talks to each of us in different ways," Father Brooke said. "Perhaps he is telling you something right now. That pane depicts the angel Gabriel's visit to the shepherds in the book of Luke. But come, you can stay in my quarters behind the church. There is a wash bin, soap, and towels for you to freshen up. Sister Agnes will find some clean clothes for the both of you."

Father Brooke lived in a humble two-room cottage about a hundred feet or so from the church. He led them inside and as he was turning to leave, Isaac grabbed his arm.

"Thank you, Father," the boy said, holding out his hand. The priest shook it and gave him a friendly clap on the back.

Joy ran over and gave the priest a hug. He smiled and kissed her on the forehead. He was gone in an instant, leaving them to revel in their good fortune.

Chapter 17

I t was nearly dark, and Father Brooke had still not returned from Fort Norfolk. Isaac began to worry something had happened to him. Sister Agnes had found Joy a new blue dress, bonnet, and stockings. Isaac was given a pair of wool pants, a clean white shirt, a blue sack coat, and kepi cap along with some stockings and a pair of brogans that had belonged to Agnes's older brother. They were a bit big for him, but beggars can't be choosers, and he figured he would grow into them.

They washed up, brushed their teeth, and felt like humans again. Isaac offered to pay for the new clothes, but Agnes would not hear of it and left them in the priest's cottage with a bag of jacks, which they amused themselves with on the floor until they tired of it. Agnes had brought them some biscuits and apples but had heard no word from Father Brooke.

As the evening wore on, with no sign of the good priest, the worry turned to grave concern. Dusk was fast settling in, and Isaac sat at the window overlooking the courtyard. He was about to go and use the latrine when he saw two riders coming up the narrow lane that led to the church. They were a rough-looking pair wearing chaps and low-brimmed hats, both with grizzled faces and bushy beards. Agnes was carrying a mop and bucket from the small woodshed and met them near the side entrance of the church.

Isaac opened the window a crack so that he could hear. Joy joined him.

"Is the parson around, deary?" the taller of the two men asked in a flirtatious voice.

Agnes was barely out of her teens, a slim girl with chestnut hair and blue eyes.

"No, sir," Agnes said. "He is out at the present. Business at Fort Norfolk. Is there something that I can do for you?" she asked nervously.

The taller man eyed his partner, who had lit a smoke and seemed to be fine with letting the other man do all the talking.

"Is he, now? Yuh wouldn't by chance have seen a boy and a young negress travelin' around abouts here, have yuh?"

"N-no, I have not. Why? Why would you ask that?"

The two men glanced at one another and this time it was the smoking man who talked. Although shorter than his companion, he was older and more compact. He pulled back his heavy coat, revealing a shiny badge.

"The boy is wanted for a murder out around Suffolk, at Jericho Plantation. Killed a man in cold blood. Boy ain't no angel, ma'am," the sheriff said, flicking off ashes from his cigarette. "He done whupped a docker over in Portsmouth and robbed a fisherman last night not a half mile from there, about killed 'em both. He's a bad one, ma'am."

"He's a sheriff!" Joy whispered.

Isaac nodded. He felt a lump in his throat.

Agnes cleared her throat and placed the bucket down in front of her along with the mop. "And how old is this boy, Sheriff?"

The sheriff removed his hat and scratched his bald head.

"Oh, I don't know. Name's Isaac Barker. If he done whupped Frank Lewis with a single punch, I say he's gotta be at least sixteen or seventeen. Frank's a prize fighter. Wil Jericho didn't say how old he is, only that he has yellow hair and is a little rough around the edges."

Isaac's mouth dropped, and he looked at his bruised knuckles, then at Joy who was chuckling lightly. He shook his head in disbelief.

"If I see him, I will be sure to let you know," Agnes said.

"Thank you, ma'am," the sheriff said, tilting his hat. "If you don't mind, I think we'll look around a bit. Nothin' like bein' too safe when yuh got rogues like this runnin' around."

Agnes watched as they headed for the church, she then made a beeline for the cottage where she found Isaac strapping on his belt and holsters.

"There is a sheriff outside looking for you. I do not believe the things he told me, but you must hide in the woods until he is gone. He is in the church now with one of his cronies. Go out the rear door!"

They grabbed their cloaks and sprinted across the grass. They found a spot among some granite boulders at the edge of the forest where they could safely observe what was happening around the church. It was now dusk, and the sun had set, leaving the western sky a blend of pink, purple, and white ribbons. They were only about a hundred feet or so from the road leading to the church. A light from a lantern glowing through the stained-glass windows told them someone was inside, searching. Did they suspect their quarry to be nearby?

The pounding of hooves told them someone was fast approaching from the road. A party of horsemen, their fierce silhouettes outlined against the twilight, galloped by, and rode into the churchyard.

Isaac immediately recognized the hulking form of Wil Jericho, along with his son Joseph, who was the first to dismount. He also spotted the man with the porkchop sideburns named Carl.

"Why do they suspect we are here?" Joy whispered.

"I don't know," Isaac replied.

That is when he thought about the boat. They had been careless in leaving it tied to that tree. He should have hidden it in the woods or let it drift back out into the river. The owner of it surely would have reported it missing, despite leaving the coins for its use, and someone must have seen it.

Either that or the steamer might have reported their near collision with a small boat. Either way, it only made sense the search for them was now being concentrated on the Norfolk side of the river and in this general area. What better place to hide than a church?

The sheriff and his deputy came back out into the churchyard where they met the Jerichos.

Wil remained mounted, but Joseph had tethered his horse to a hitching rail and lit a cigarette, the tip glowing like a hot coal in the darkness.

"They found the boat tied to a sapling. It is the crabber's boat that went missing," Joseph said to the sheriff, puffing on his cigarette.

"They are around here somewhere, then," the sheriff said. "This little nun knows more'n she tellin' us," he added. "Acted really nervous."

Wil dismounted and handed the reins of his horse to one of his men.

"War is this little lady right now? I think ah'll have a word with her," Wil said.

The sheriff motioned with his thumb toward the priest's house. "She was headed to that cottage with a mop and bucket. The priest is at Fort Norfolk."

Wil's face dropped. "Fort Norfolk? What business does a priest have at Fort Norfolk, Sheriff?"

The sheriff shrugged. "I don't rightly know, Wil. Perhaps he's gone over there tuh save some souls. Yuh know how unrighteous some of them soldiers and sailors are, always visitin' them houses of ill repute and all."

"No. Ah don't think that's it, Sheriff," Wil responded angrily. "Isaac Barker has a friend over thar by the name of Major Frost. Charles Braxton told me this. I suspect that the boy is tryin' tuh find him."

Wil stormed off toward the cottage with the loyal Carl at his heels. Isaac did not trust the pair would be civil with Agnes. If he detected anything that might suggest the young nun was in trouble, he would come to her aid. There was no way he would let a lady be terrified by a pair such as these without attempting to come to her rescue.

The sheriff and Joseph walked around the church out of sight and hearing. Isaac wondered what had happened to Father Brooke. Was he still at the fort? Perhaps he was waiting for Major Frost to return? He thought about the possibilities but could not come to any conclusions.

A few minutes elapsed in tense anticipation when, finally, Joy nudged Isaac on the shoulder and pointed toward the front of the church. The sheriff was returning with Joseph after their private conversation. The lawman mounted his steed and, along with his deputy, disappeared into the night, leaving the Jericho party alone at the church.

Isaac began to worry about Agnes. He knew what kind of man Wil Jericho was and could only imagine Carl was of the same disposition. He could see Joseph urinating against the side of church just beneath the stained glass of the shepherd. A wave of anger washed over him as he watched this blasphemous act, and he felt himself clenching his fists.

Joseph lit another cigarette and started for the cottage just as Wil and Carl emerged. Wil was holding a lantern in one hand and the bag of jacks Isaac and Joy had been playing with in the other. He tossed it to Joseph. "What do yuh think of a parson that plays with jacks?"

Joseph briefly studied the bag and then dropped it on the grass. He took a drag from his cigarette, blowing two jets from his nose.

"I think we need tuh wait on this parson tuh return. You check that place good, Pa?"

"'Course, son. If they are 'round here, they haven't gotten far. The missus ain't talkin', and she told us we are no longer welcome here. What do yuh think about that?"

Wil turned to Carl. "We gonna ride out tuh Fort Norfolk. Stay here and keep an eye on the sister. I suspect she knows where these children are, and ah don't want her tuh give them a nod, if yuh get my meanin'."

Carl growled something in response, but what it was, Isaac could not hear. He then watched the Jericho party, minus Carl, ride off down the road in the direction of Fort Norfolk. Joy tapped Isaac on the wrist. She was pointing at Carl, who was heading back toward the cottage just as Agnes appeared in the doorway. She was holding the bucket and mop and noticed the burly man approaching, spurs jingling as he walked. She tried to brush by him, but he turned with her and followed her toward the church.

"War is thet boy, Sister?"

She hurried into the church through the side door, attempting to get away from him, but he followed her inside.

"Is it true what they say about all you nuns? Yuh can't tell lies, right?" Carl asked, grabbing Agnes's wrist and pushing her up against the altar.

Agnes twisted out of his grasp, but he grabbed her and once again pushed her back against the altar. She could smell his rancid breath.

"Now tell me where that murderin' boy is, woman. I know he is around here somewar and I intend tuh collect the bounty.

"Please! This is a house of God!" she screamed.

239

He slapped her, brushing away the silver candlesticks, which clanked onto the stone floor. The church was lit by a dozen votive candles set in a stepped tray under a marble statue of the Madonna. He never saw the candlestick that connected with his skull and sent him sprawling unconscious onto the flagstones behind the altar. Isaac stood over him with his Colt drawn, the kepi low on his head. When he was satisfied that the brute was out cold, he disarmed him and wrapped his ankles together with his own belt. With a herculean effort, he dragged the big man from the church out into the courtyard where he lashed him to a tree with some rope that he found in the woodshed. He then returned to the church where he found Joy with Agnes sitting in one of the pews. The young nun was crying as Joy did her best to comfort her.

"Is he alive?" Agnes asked, tears streaming down her red cheeks. Joy cradled her head and was wiping her tears with her handkerchief.

"Yes, Sister Agnes," Isaac responded. "He'll have a headache for sure, but I couldn't let him do you any mischief. He's lucky I didn't end his days for the way that scoundrel was treating you, ma'am."

"Oh...oh, no, Isaac, you must not say such things. You are but a boy. Oh, where is Father Brooke?"

"He'll be here," Joy said. "In the meantime, we will stay right here with you, Sister Agnes."

Joy glanced at Isaac who was kneeling in front of the stricken nun with a heavy face.

Suddenly, the door to the church opened and Isaac's hand instinctively reached for the butt of his Colt. He breathed a sigh of relief when he saw the good priest walking quickly up the aisle.

"Dear God, what has happened in my absence? Why is there a man tied to a tree outside?"

Isaac pointed to Agnes who, overcome with emotion, rushed to the priest and threw her arms around him.

"Oh...oh, Father Brooke, it was terrible. These men came looking for Isaac and Joy. They all left, except for that one who is outside. He was trying to get me to tell him where Isaac and Joy were."

The priest's face was contorted with horror. He glanced at Joy and then Isaac.

"Children, where did these other men go?"

"They went looking for you, Father," Joy said. "They were suspicious that you were hiding us someplace. They found the boat down by the river."

Isaac was sitting in the pew with his head buried in his hands. He looked up. "Sir, I have brought you nothing but trouble. We will leave forthright so that when they return you can be truthful with them. Perhaps tell them you did not know I was a fugitive. I am grateful for all you have done for us, but look at poor Agnes, here. She has been—"

The priest stepped forward and placed a comforting hand on the boy's shoulder.

"Nonsense. I will not turn you out to the wolves. You have entered a house of God and are safe here. This is a sanctuary from those who seek to do you harm and you shall stay. I have talked to a captain at Fort Norfolk. Major Frost, who you have told me about, is across the river in search of you. The captain has sent a runner to find him and bring him here. Your troubles are almost at an end. You only need to wait. But in the meantime, what to do about he who sits bound to the tree in the courtyard? We must free him. I will order him to leave the premises."

Isaac's eyes narrowed.

"Father, that man is a scoundrel of the first order. We cannot let him go. I fear for Sister Agnes and Joy, should he get free."

The priest frowned. "Well, you are a noble boy, Isaac, with chivalric notions, but we cannot leave him there indefinitely. Perhaps it would be for the best if I went to fetch the sheriff and let him decide the man's fate."

Isaac weighed his options. Major Frost would eventually get word that Isaac and Joy were at the church. He could stay here, but the Jerichos would almost certainly arrive before the good major. In hindsight, they should have accompanied Father Brooke to the fort, but it would have been a risky adventure during the daytime. At night, however, Isaac was confident in his abilities. They could stick to the shadows of the roadway and detect any movement approaching from either direction.

"Father, I have an idea. If you can direct me to the fort, I will take Joy with me. We cannot stay at the church, as the Jerichos will be returning before Major Frost even gets word we are here. You can fetch the sheriff and relate all that has transpired here tonight, but Sister Agnes must go with you. These people aren't to be trusted, sir."

The priest seemed to ponder these possibilities and realized Isaac was right. He would take Agnes to the Holton farm and have Holton's boy ride into Norfolk to get the sheriff. He gave Isaac specific directions to Fort Norfolk. They would be taking the same road until it forked, but from there Isaac and Joy would take a small path that ran along the riverbank until they reached the fort. There was a road that led there, but Father Brooke reasoned that would be the way the Jerichos would be returning from. There was an open grassy plain and sand dunes where the path ended and the good priest warned them it would be their most dangerous part of the trek, as there would be nowhere to hide or conceal themselves should they get caught on open ground.

The short walk to the forks was uneventful and the two parties took their leave of one another with well wishes. Father Brooke had told them exactly where the path was located and Joy, with her eagle eyes, was the first to spot it.

It was pitch dark and the sounds of the river lent an ominous vibe to the chilly night. At one point the trail merged with the sandy shore of the riverbank as the good priest said it would. They found themselves bathed by the moonlight that sent a distorted, rippling glare across the water.

Somewhere, a fish jumped, causing a loud splash that had Isaac reaching for his Colt.

They might have been halfway to the fort when a single horseman appeared out of the woods onto the beach in front of them, followed closely by a second rider whose horse whinnied and nudged ahead of the first horseman. The two riders sat astride their mounts for a few seconds, gazing at the shadowy figures of Isaac and Joy before breaking into a canter and heading straight at them.

Chapter 18

Isaac grabbed Joy's hand and made a mad dash into the woods, reasoning correctly that the horses could not follow. In the moonlight, he caught a quick glimpse of their pursuers and recognized the two men as being the sheriff and his tall deputy. They had obviously been to the fort and were returning by way of the path instead of using the main road.

"Stop! In the name of the law!" came a voice behind them.

Isaac cursed their luck. He had assumed the sheriff and his deputy had ridden back into the city proper. He had not considered they might have gone to Fort Norfolk. *Well*, he thought, *they will have a hard time finding us in the woods in the dark.*

Isaac could hear the heavy tread of their pursuers behind them, the crispy leaves crunching under their boots. If these were bounty hunters, Isaac would not hesitate to use his Colt or derringer, but these were lawmen. He would respect that until they gave him reason not to.

The two youths were easily putting distance between themselves and the sheriff when the unexpected happened. Joy became faint and realized with horror that she was having one of her spells. Collapsing next to an aged white pine, she grabbed her head and closed her eyes.

"Oh, Isaac. I am having another one. I think it is a bad one. Leave me here and go! You must get away or they will hang you!"

Isaac could feel his heart racing. His instinct told him to run. However, there was no way he was leaving her, regardless of what might happen to him. He sat down next to her and cradled her head in his lap. She could feel the warmth of his hands as he tried to massage her temples to ease the pain.

"I'm not leaving you, Joy. We either get out of this together or not at all. Now, let us be real quiet and maybe, just maybe, they will miss us in the darkness."

For a few minutes they sat in silence, listening to the sounds of the forest. A nearby warbler with its metallic notes chirped away until it abruptly stopped. The reason, Isaac knew, was that it detected a threat. Then he heard footsteps. They came nearer until he looked up and saw the shadowy figure of the tall deputy glaring at him. He was holding his revolver on them and wearing a smug look.

"Let's see those hands, boy. Nice and slow."

"The girl is sick and needs my help," Isaac muttered. He was desperate. He could feel Joy's shallow breathing. Her eyes were closed, her face set in a painful grimace.

"I don't give a damn about no slave girl!"

The deputy cocked his head to the side. "Sheriff! I got them dead to rahts over here!"

Isaac felt Joy's hand touching his. "I-Isaac, it is no use. Go with them. Maybe, just maybe, the major will help you."

The sheriff arrived, out of breath. Despite the temperature, he was sweating buckets. There was a look of satisfaction on his face when he saw the two fugitives. However, he was also baffled. From all the stories floating around, he had imagined the boy to be a stout youth of sixteen or seventeen, not a waif-like boy of twelve or thirteen. It was no matter to him. He finally had his quarry.

"Get up!" he ordered, pulling his pistol from its holster. "Unless yuh want me tuh put a bullet in that little pixie's head."

Isaac swallowed hard and stood up with his hands raised.

"Sheriff, she is sick. Please—"

The sheriff interrupted him. "Shut your mouth, boy. I haven't had a wink of sleep in near forty-eight hours cuz o' you and all it might take is a smart mouth fer me tuh pull this trigger."

The deputy grabbed Isaac by his collar and slammed him up against a tree. He was quickly dispossessed of his weapons and his wrists were cuffed behind him, the iron biting into his skin causing him to wince in pain. The deputy pushed him along but when Isaac noticed they were leaving Joy behind, he panicked.

"You can't leave her, Sheriff! She's sick. She will die out here in the cold!"

"Let her die then," came the callous response. "The coyotes and the buzzards will have a feast."

The deputy snickered. "She too skinny, Sheriff. The coyotes will let the worms and bugs git her!"

Isaac felt his blood boiling. Somehow, he managed to struggle out of the deputy's firm grip and bolt back to where Joy sat, her eyes glazed and dilated.

Her head was throbbing. She had lost all sense of hearing and what she saw next seemed to be something out of a nightmare. She could see

Isaac's mouth moving, his teary eyes fixed on her as he hit the ground with the deputy on top of him. Then, mercifully, she passed out.

****

She awoke sometime later. At first, she was disoriented, her eyes darting back and forth in the darkness. Surprisingly, she was no longer cold and ascertained the reason why. She was wrapped up in a warm saddle blanket next to a blazing campfire. She sat up. Glancing around her, she could see a boy sitting on a rock. He was holding a stick with a piece of meat attached to it, letting it roast over the flames.

"I-Isaac?"

The boy looked surprised and rushed over to her. "Joy, thank God! Praise the Lord!"

He held a canteen to her lips, and she took a few sips. She wiped her lips with the back of her hand. "Elijah? But how?"

"It's me, Joy! And don't worry none about Isaac. I have a plan!"

"How did you know where to find me?"

Elijah clasped Joy's hands in his, a bright smile on his battered and bruised face.

250

"Joy, after I left you and Isaac, I made my way to Suffolk and sent that message to Major Frost. I was about to head back home when what do my eyes fall upon, but good old faithful Betsy! Apparently, some trader found her grazing in the pasture outside of town. I claimed her as mine and decided this good luck was your good luck. I decided tuh ride tuh Fort Norfolk myself. I got thar in no time at all, but Major Frost had already left the fort with a company of men. They were out searchin' for yuh. I decided I would wait for him to return. Well, word got around that you and Isaac were seen over in Norfolk. The major still hadn't returned last night when Sheriff Connors and that cutthroat deputy showed up looking for some priest. Well, I decided tuh follow them and kept a good distance away. That's when I saw their horses tethered to a tree down by the river, and a few minutes later here they come with Isaac screaming his bloody head off. By God, Joy, Isaac's got the courage of ten grown men!"

Joy listened to Elijah's story with fascination and then she related all their adventures since he had left them nearly two days before. She was still weak, but nothing was going to stop her from trying to get back to Isaac. It was all she was able to think about. "And what is your plan, Elijah?"

The boy had forgotten his meat and when he pulled the burning stick out of the flames with the charred piece of rabbit attached to it, he burst out laughing but then suddenly became serious. Once again, he squatted in front of Joy. "Joy, we gonna bust him outta jail!"

Joy's eyes widened, her mouth forming a perfect circle. "Uh...we gonna do what, Elijah?"

"Yuh heard me right, Joy," the boy said with a chuckle. "I got it all figured out. Yuh see, Sheriff Connors and Deputy Colson know me. They know my family. My evil pa was the one that got them their jobs. So, really, they are indebted to the Jerichos. We will walk right intuh that jail. I'll make up this story and tell them that I found yuh wanderin' around down by the river and ah'm takin' yuh back to Jericho Plantation."

Joy was interested, but she still had no idea how they would free Isaac. "Elijah, that's all fine, but Isaac will be locked up. I don't see how—"

He stopped her. "I'm getting tuh that, Joy. Wait until yuh hear how we are gonna get him out!"

She played along. "All right, how are we going to do it?"

"So, the sheriff will take one good look at muh face and say, 'What the hell happened tuh you, boy?' And I'll tell him that Isaac Barker whupped me and I'm here tuh get muh revenge. He lets me in the cell. In the meantime, Joy, you distract the sheriff with small talk. We pretend Isaac whups me yet again and disarms me. Isaac will come out of the cell holdin' my pistol up tuh muh head. So, while I am a hostage, Isaac threatens tuh blow muh brains out unless he lets yuh lock the sheriff in the cell."

Joy was looking at Elijah with an inquisitive frown, her big brown eyes blinking. Then a smile started at the corner of her mouth before spreading rapidly across her face. She burst out laughing and Elijah cocked an eyebrow.

"What's the matter? Yuh don't think it will work?"

She sat bolt upright. Her indomitable energy had returned. "Elijah, we are going to make it work," she said, gripping his shoulders. "Let's go!"

She struggled to her feet and staggered slightly. Elijah caught her before she fell and helped her sit down.

"Now, Joy, we gotta wait until at least sunrise. Yuh just had a bad spell. We can't do nothin' until daybreak anyhow."

She held her small hands out toward the fire, absorbing its warmth. "We must have a backup plan, Elijah. What if the sheriff isn't there and his deputy is? Or they might both be there? What if he lets you into the cell and wishes to see you deliver Isaac a beating? Then what? He will know it is all a ruse because you won't have time to tell Isaac what is going on. The distraction must happen just after he lets you in the cell."

Elijah was scratching his ear, his mouth twisted in a grimace. He hadn't thought about that. "Darn it, Joy. Now I'm puzzled!"

"I'm just thinking of all the possibilities, that's all," she said, shaking her head. "We are only going to have one chance and we will have to get it right."

After a few seconds of contemplation, Joy clapped her hands. "I got it, Elijah! You will go inside first. I will wait outside for a minute and then start banging on the door. The sheriff will naturally leave you and Isaac to see what all the fuss is about. That will be your opportunity to cue Isaac in on the plan. When the sheriff returns, Isaac will have you as a hostage and I will lock the sheriff in the cell."

Elijah held up two fingers. "But what if there are two lawmen?"

Joy placed her index finger and thumb on her chin. "Well, somehow, I will distract them both. You leave that to me. I am pretty sharp when it comes to figuring out these things, Elijah. The most important thing is that he lets you in the cell or our whole plan will fail. Now, how will you let me know you are in the cell?"

Elijah frowned. "Yeah. That'll be the tricky part, Joy."

"Is there a window or any other place where I might be able to hear what is going on?" she asked.

His face brightened. "It is a two-cell jail. Ah've been thar with Joseph a few times. If ah remember raht, thar is a barred window high up on the stone wall in each cell. Once yuh hear me yell, 'Ah'm gonna whup yuh, Isaac!' that is your cue. Now, be quick, yuh hear. Isaac might think ah done gone crazy and he might really whup me! Don't think ah wanna rough and tumble with Isaac. Ah done hear he knocked out Frank Lewis with a single punch! Dang it, Joy, Frank's twice his size! Ah wish ah'd seen that!"

Joy smiled, reflecting on how cool and collected Isaac had been in the time since they set out three days before. Isaac had reasoned correctly. He was driven by a sense of purpose mixed with courage and determination. It had gotten them through. Now it was up to her and Elijah to get him out of this fix and that is exactly what she was going to do.

She just prayed she would not have another one of her spells.

Chapter 19

Isaac was miserable. He sat on a filthy straw mattress in his cell staring blankly at the whitewashed stone walls. The place reeked of urine and feces. A pail, caked with excrement, sat in the corner of the small room. It was here, he was told, he could relieve himself should the need arise.

He felt nauseous and his head ached terribly from the deputy slamming his head into the dirt as he attempted to get to Joy. He looked up at the barred window, high up on the wall. The morning light shot through it, casting a beam onto the floor where he could see dust particles floating freely in the stagnant air. He had tested the bars of his cell. They appeared old and crusty, but they were firmly attached. There was no way out. He was locked up tight.

The sheriff and the deputy had shoved him into the cell hours earlier, and he had not seen them since. He had screamed at them and hurled insults, but they had ignored his protests. Finally, he had succumbed to exhaustion, crying himself to sleep. When he awoke, it was daylight.

He thought about Joy and the way they had just left her there in the cold to die, as if she were some kind of animal. If he ever got out of this, he would make them pay. He swore to it and was determined they would all be brought to justice. He did not understand how anyone could be so cruel. He still had hope, of course. Major Frost was out there somewhere and would soon learn, if he hadn't already, that he had been captured.

There was also the chance Joy was still alive. He prayed the spell had passed and she was able to get somewhere warm. It was all he could do while he sat there languishing in the empty cell.

He stood up and staggered over to the door of his cell. The bars were almost wide enough for his slender frame to fit through. He cursed and pounded his fist against the iron. He was cold. They had taken his cloak and coat, leaving him in his shirtsleeves. They had even stolen his pocket watch and all his money. He heard a door opening and the deputy appeared. He was grinning, holding a cup of water and a piece of stale crust in one hand and a set of jingling jailer's keys in the other. He fit the key into the lock and swung the door open.

"Your Majesty, breakfast is served," he said, dropping the crust in the disgusting pail and placing the cup of water on the floor next to it. "Eat up. Yuh won't get another until this evening, yuh murderin' little devil," he said with a smile.

For a few seconds, Isaac stared at the water and the bread which had landed on a hard brown lump in the pail. Deputy Colson was watching his reaction. Isaac figured he was looking for an excuse to rough him up. Isaac, however, did not take the bait. Instead, he merely picked the crust out of the pail and tossed it against the wall. The deputy's face lost all its humor.

The deputy slammed the door shut and turned the key, leaving Isaac to do as he pleased in his isolation. The boy looked up at the barred window. It was at least eight feet above the floor. Even if he stood on the folded mattress, using the pail as a step he would not come close to reaching it.

In the adjacent cell Isaac could hear but not see someone snoring. He sat down on the mattress and buried his head in his hands. An hour or so passed and he kept going over the events of the previous few weeks. He began to wonder about the things he might have done differently. If Charles Braxton had not gotten in their way, he was convinced he could have gotten Joy to the train station, and they could have somehow ridden the rails into Norfolk. He got up and kicked the pail across the cell in frustration, knocking over his cup of water in the process. He then heard voices beyond the door and then Deputy Colson cackling. The door opened and he was shocked to see Elijah

Jericho emerge into the hallway, followed by the deputy who was wearing a broad smirk.

"Elijah?"

The deputy opened the cell, letting Elijah in. The older boy was cracking his knuckles.

"I'm gonna whup yuh, Isaac!"

Isaac was confused. He backed up as Elijah slowly advanced toward him. Suddenly, there was a violent racket near the front of the jail and the unmistakable sound of shattering glass.

Deputy Colson turned. "What in the name of...?" He rushed from the room to see what had just happened, forgetting the opened cell door with his keys hanging from the lock.

Elijah pulled his pocket pistol from its holster.

Isaac was shocked. "Elijah, what...what are you doing?"

"Relax, Isaac. Me and Joy are bustin' yuh outta here. Now, take this pistol and hold it up tuh muh head. Yuh gonna take me as a hostage so we can get outta here."

Isaac felt overwhelmed. "Joy? She...she's outside?"

Elijah cracked a smile. "Yes. Now hurry. We have tuh be convincing."

Isaac took the pistol and grabbed Elijah around the neck. Together they exited the cell and entered the office part of the jail where Deputy Colson was inspecting the shards of glass all over the floor. He had gone outside but did not notice Joy.

A look of horror washed over the deputy's face when he saw Isaac with the muzzle of the pistol against Elijah's temple.

"He's gonna kill me, Deputy Colson! This dang Yankee boy here is crazy!" Elijah screamed.

Isaac waved his pistol at the deputy. "You better do as I say, or he gets it through the brains! Now move!"

He motioned with the pistol toward the door that led to the cells and when the deputy was inside, Joy appeared like a ghost and slammed the door shut, quickly turning the key.

"Boy, yuh better put that pistol down and let me outta this cell or thar is gonna be hell tuh pay!"

Isaac lowered the pistol and let go of Elijah who clapped his cousin on the back. Joy was still holding the jailer's keys and, with a smug expression, dropped them on the floor just outside of the deputy's reach. Isaac reached over and grabbed Joy around the waist and kissed her on the cheek. They were both so happy, their eyes filled with tears.

"Oh! Joy...I...thought you were dead! Thank God!"

Deputy Colson was gripping the bars of the cell so tight his knuckles had turned white. "What the hell is goin' on? Elijah Jericho, yore daddy ain't gonna like this! Now, let me outta this cell!"

"I really don't much care what muh daddy likes, Deputy. Far as ah'm concerned, he ain't muh daddy no more." Elijah turned to Isaac. "Come on, cousin, let's git outta here."

They turned heel and could hear the deputy's curses as Joy slammed the door behind them. Once in the office, Isaac found his belt and weapons on the sheriff's desk, along with his sack coat and cloak. After rearming himself, he headed out into the cold morning, followed by Joy and Elijah. There was a stiff breeze blowing, and Elijah led them to the hitching post where he and Joy had left Betsy.

"It's a gonna be a tight squeeze," Elijah said with a grin, "but ol' Betsy can handle the three of us lightweights fer sure."

Elijah took the reins, with Joy in the middle and Isaac taking the rear. They were soon galloping down the road in the direction of Fort Norfolk. They were almost at the forks when they spotted a party of six horsemen on the other road. If they kept coming, they would pass each other right at the junction.

"Dang it! That's Pa and his bunch!" Elijah exclaimed, drawing in the reins, and racing off toward the south.

"Do you think they saw us?" Joy asked.

"Well, maybe. But they have no idea that ah'm in town unless someone at the fort told 'em. As far as you and Isaac, they probably think you are dead and that Isaac is still locked tightly in his cell."

They turned and came up to a large warehouse, passing a row of docker houses. They were almost to the bridge leading back into the city when they saw another party of horses coming at them on the other side. They were trapped. Desperate to find a place to hide, Elijah turned back and headed for the wharf.

"We will be hemmed in!" Isaac exclaimed.

Isaac looked behind him and noticed the original party of horsemen had split up. Two of the riders were heading toward them, obviously with the intention of discerning who they were. The other four kept the course toward the bridge. Joy tapped Elijah on the shoulder and pointed toward a quartet of small boats tied to mooring masts.

"That's our chance!"

Elijah immediately ascertained what Joy's plan was and headed for the boats. They chose a small one with three benches and two sets of paddles. Isaac untied the mooring rope while Elijah set Betsy free. She was a good horse, but they couldn't take her on the boat.

Joy sat on the small seat in the front while Isaac took the oars in the middle, and Elijah the ones in the rear. Just as they pushed away from the dock the two riders arrived, and Isaac recognized them immediately as Joseph Jericho and the rogue, Carl. Apparently, Father Brooke had not convinced the sheriff the man was a scoundrel. Of course, it was not hard to see why. He was in the pay of the Jerichos, who owned the sheriff and his offices.

Carl immediately set off to fetch Wil Jericho, who was riding with the sheriff and the others. Joseph followed the boat along the shoreline, all the while hurling expletives and profanities at the trio who were slowly rowing up the channel toward the fort.

"They are going to beat us to the fort, Elijah," Isaac grunted, pulling hard on the oars.

"Dang it, don't I know it," Elijah said in a winded voice. "But surely it'll git the attention of the soldiers. Major Frost left Captain Rogers in charge at the fort, and he'll surely come tuh our assistance."

Joy pointed toward the shoreline. "Elijah, it's that sheriff with your pa!"

The two boys rowed until their muscles were burning. There was no way they were going to make it to the fort before the horses.

It was then that Joy had an idea. If they could fire a shot when they got close to the fort, perhaps they would get the attention of the garrison. Possibly, they would come out to meet them. Isaac and Elijah thought it was a capital idea and decided to do just that. The two boys took turns laying in the oars and resting.

The constant rowing paid off and the trio of fugitives were soon within sight of the massive seawall of the fort. Fort Norfolk was an impressive sight. It was designed in the classic shape of a star with the recent addition of a ravelin to protect the garrison from a land assault. Of course, from their perspective, they could only see the top of the barracks and gatehouse rising above the seawall.

There was a grassy slope that led down to the beach, and it was here that the party of Wil Jericho waited for their arrival.

"Maybe we should row across the river, Isaac," Elijah said nervously. He could see his father mounted on his large destrier, coolly smoking a cigar, and he felt a wave of panic overcome him. He wanted no part of the man, but it appeared a confrontation was inevitable.

Isaac, too, had considered fleeing toward the Portsmouth shore but realized the futility of it.

"We would never make it, Elijah. The current would take us out into the bay. As it is, we are going to have a whirl of a time getting to the beach. Let's head for the point."

Isaac pulled his Colt from his holster and without aiming it, pulled the trigger, firing a single shot into the air, the bullet landing harmlessly in the sea behind them. He still had four rounds left in the Colt and a single shot in the derringer. He could see the fear on Elijah's face, but Joy seemed to be content.

"I...I don't like it, Isaac. Mebbe we should steer for the bay," Elijah said into the wind.

Isaac shook his head. "Is your Colt loaded?" he asked, perturbed that the boy, who had shown so much courage in breaking him out of jail, was now going yellow on him.

"It is. Five shots."

"Well," Isaac said, pulling hard on the oars, "we might need you to use it. I'm not running anymore. Your pa hates you because you are a good person. You're not like him. I'm proud to call you my cousin, Elijah."

Joy reached over and touched Elijah's hand. He had quit rowing and was peering nervously at the shoreline.

"You're not going to face him alone, Elijah," Joy said. "We will be there right next to you. They will be reluctant to shoot us down like dogs, especially with all those soldiers and sailors as witnesses."

Elijah was fidgeting in his seat, but Isaac noticed a slight grin wash over his bruised face.

"Awright, then," the older boy said with confidence. "Let's head for that patch of woods. They can't get the horses in thar and will have tuh go in on foot. We might be able tuh lose them and skirt around the fort and come in on the land side."

They all agreed with Elijah's plan and set it in motion. A couple of sailors had come out onto the seawall to have a look. They had obviously heard Isaac's shot and would have by now seen the party of horsemen following the small boat along the beach. One of the riders was hollering into the wind but the occupants of the boat were too far away to hear what he was saying.

The small boat struck the rocky bottom a few feet from the shore and Isaac jumped knee-deep into the water. He helped Joy onto solid ground without getting her feet wet. They had landed in a thick tangle of loblolly pines and elderberry bushes, and it was all they could do to work their way through them. They could hear voices to the east, but their plan seemed to be working. Isaac and Joy followed Elijah, as he had been to the fort numerous times and knew the layout well.

"The danger will be the open ground when we emerge from this here wood," Elijah said. "Undoubtedly, some of Pa's men will be ridin' around lookin' tuh see where we might come out and some'll be searchin' the wood."

They came to a clearing and darted past an old well and that is when the horsemen came down on them. Rounding the stone palisade of the fort's outer works came three riders. In the lead, the fearsome form of Wil Jericho sat tall in his saddle. It had come to this. And Isaac was ready.

Chapter 20

For a few seconds there was a whirlwind of confusion as the three horsemen chased down the three fugitives who had retreated to the well. Isaac and Elijah had brandished their revolvers, letting their antagonists know they were not going to be taken willingly. Joy kept close to Isaac. She felt a headache coming on but some innate power within her prevented it from consuming her. It was as if she were willing it away, knowing what was at stake.

The three horsemen, which included Wil Jericho and his man, Carl, along with another rough-looking member of the posse, circled the trio at a safe distance. Wil was chewing on a cigar. He was not worried about his son. He had always been able to intimidate and belittle him.

Isaac Barker, on the other hand, was a different matter. He had been a hard nut to crack. Thus far, he had been elusive and, though still a boy, he had shown obstinate determination and fortitude in being able to avoid capture. Those who had grappled with him had all been overcome. It was as if some divine force was at work assisting him in his endeavor to whisk Joy away to freedom. However, Wil Jericho did not believe in divine intervention. Neither did he believe in fate. Isaac

Barker, to him, had been an impediment to something material he yearned to have.

Times were changing. Civil War loomed on the horizon and his desire to extend his influence in the region by purchasing great tracts of land would make him a rich man. Not that he was not already wealthy. Indeed, he had enough assets in land, but recently he had been hurting. A series of bad crops had forced him to sell nearly half of his slaves and therefore neglect a good many of his fields.

He wanted to be one of the shakers and movers. It was greed that led him to murder, and now a young boy and a slave girl threatened to expose his guilt. That could not happen. He needed Raymond Barker's estate, and no upstart youngster was going to threaten that.

If only his idiotic cousin Charles had not gotten drunk, but then, it had been his own fault Isaac Barker was even in Virginia. He had needed a cover, a pretext for having poor old Uncle Raymond's will brought to him in time to have it forged and presented to the probate court. He had thought of everything, except for one thing. He had underestimated Isaac and was now forced to reckon with his problem.

Wil reined in his horse, the destrier prancing a good thirty feet from his quarry. "Elijah, put down your gun, boy. Ah didn't mean all the bad things ah told yuh the other day. Joseph done gathered up Betsy and yuh can ride back with us. Ah'll even get yuh another Colt. A real Navy model this time. Whatcha say, boy?"

"He's not going with you, swine!" Isaac bellowed. "You're a murderer and I am going to see that you pay for your crime!"

Wil felt his hardened face turning red with anger. He threw his cigar on the ground and pointed at Isaac, his finger wagging back and forth.

"Ah am not talkin' tuh you, boy. You're going tuh the hangman's noose when we are done here."

Joy stepped forward. She had heard enough, and Wil Jericho no longer intimidated her. In fact, she felt no fear. Standing as tall as her small frame allowed with her hands on her hips, she was going to be heard.

"He is not going to the hangman's noose, Wil Jericho. If anyone is, you are! We know all about the forged will and your involvement in the murder of Isaac's uncle. I heard you talking about it with Joseph and that man who tried to whip me. I'm going to testify in court to it and there is nothing you can do to stop me."

Wil shifted uncomfortably in his saddle and leaned forward, glaring at the young girl who had not moved an inch. "Testify in court? You are my slave, girl! Mother Etta has spoiled yuh rotten and given yuh evil notions. Now, the best thing yuh can do is be a good little slave and go with Elijah so's I can deal with this ruffian that has kidnapped muh property! Because, girl, yuh are muh property. Make no mistake about that!"

Isaac felt his fingers tightening on the butt of his Colt. He wanted nothing more than to shoot this man out of his saddle, but that would not do. The man on the horse would have to make the first move and then he would let him have it. In his peripheral vision, he could see the bulky form of Carl trying to be sneaky and get behind them, but their backs were against the well. The third man was a young, cadaverous-looking fellow with a beak-shaped nose. He was smoking a cigarette and carrying a flint lock carbine in a sling ring.

For a few seconds no one spoke. Isaac was keeping a close watch on their three antagonists, especially Beak Nose, who had removed his carbine from the ring and laid it across the pommel of his horse. Finally, it was Wil who spoke, addressing Joy, who had stepped back next to Isaac.

"Since you belong tuh me, girlie, ah have the right tuh do anything ah want tuh yuh, and ah think ah'll start right now with a whipping."

Wil motioned for the sycophantic Carl to come alongside him and hold his horse. He then dismounted and pulled out a cat o' nine tails that was attached to his saddle. He ran his thick, stubby fingers over the braids and, with a wicked grin, advanced toward the girl, who naturally gravitated toward Isaac for protection. The boy pushed her behind him and held his Colt level against the grinning monster, who stopped when he noticed the level of intensity in Isaac's eyes.

"You wouldn't shoot me, boy. You'll soon have the rest of the posse and the sheriff bearin' down on yuh. That would be rather stupid, now, wouldn't it?"

Isaac was biting on his lower lip, his fingers twitching nervously. "You take another step, mister, and I'll send you straight to hell. You can bet on it!"

Elijah took a step toward his father in a last-ditch attempt to reason with him. "Pa, let's talk about this. Please!"

The whip shot out, taking Elijah off guard, and striking him a glancing blow across his neck, but it was enough to knock him down, his Colt flying from his hand. What happened next happened so fast Isaac had a hard time recalling it. Wil raised the whip again, this time aiming for Isaac and Joy, his eyes red with rage as he let it fly, but Isaac was too fast. Throwing Joy to the ground he took the brunt of the knotted cord on his back, but the cloak protected him from what would have been a painful delivery. He then spun around with his Colt and aimed at his attacker's abdomen. Wil had unholstered his pistol and brought it up, but Isaac's bullet entered his stomach before the scoundrel could get a shot off.

"Yuh shot me!" Wil exclaimed with horror. He had dropped to his knees and was holding his stomach, gazing down at the dark blood seeping through his fingers.

Isaac, however, did not have time to discuss matters with the stricken man, he heard the flintlock's hammer being cocked and, dropping to one knee, he wheeled around and fired just as Beak Nose was leveling his carbine at him. The bullet blasted through his attacker's neck and windpipe, knocking the thin man off his horse, the carbine landing harmlessly a few feet away. Isaac then turned to the cowardly Carl who was still holding his master's horse.

"Get off that horse!" the boy ordered, holding his Colt in front of him. Carl was shaking, his fat body fidgeting nervously in the saddle. He was staring in disbelief at the prone form of Wil Jericho who had slumped over onto his side and was groaning in agony. With some effort he climbed down from his horse and held his hands up. He wanted no part of Isaac Barker's Colt.

"Not so brazen now when you aren't attacking defenseless women, are you? Unhook your belt and let it drop to the ground and back up five paces," Isaac ordered, waving his Colt at him.

Carl wisely did as he was told.

Joy had rushed over to Elijah, who was sitting up holding his neck which was bleeding from the hooks that his father had threaded into the cat o' nine tails. Suddenly, there was the sound of pounding hooves and a party of horsemen crashed through the trees north of the fort. Isaac recognized Sheriff Connors and Joseph Jericho among the throng. It was too late to make a run for the fort. He could only hope the soldiers had heard the shooting.

"Pa!" Joseph screamed, leaping from his horse. The sheriff and the other riders surrounded Isaac, who was still holding the Colt on Carl.

"Put the pistol down, boy!" the sheriff ordered as he scanned the carnage around him. Isaac dropped the Colt in front of him and raised his hands, not anxious to feel a slug from one of the posse's weapons.

Joy rushed up to the sheriff, who had dismounted and was advancing toward Isaac with a reddened face. She dropped to her knees, grabbing his leg, and looking up at him with pleading eyes. "Please, Sheriff! It was self-defense! Ask Elijah. He can speak for him! Please don't hurt him!"

The sheriff reached down and grabbed Joy by the hood of her cloak and threw her to the ground. He had pulled out his cudgel and, reaching Isaac, struck him a glancing blow that landed near the base of his skull. It would probably have been a fatal blow had Isaac not reacted quickly and attempted to dodge away from it. He fell to the grass with the sheriff standing over him, the cudgel raised, ready for another blow when a dozen soldiers riding war horses came charging around the corner of the palisade.

"You strike that boy one more time and I'll end your days!" came the strong voice of Major Frost.

Joy had crawled over to Isaac and covered him with her slim body. She was determined and willing to take the blows meant for him. Her big brown eyes were glassy and filled with tears, pleading, and gazing up at the sheriff who was still

276

holding the cudgel but staring straight at the muzzle of the good major's carbine.

Isaac started to stir. Joy was cradling his head in her lap, and he was looking up at her, consciousness only now coming back to him as she stroked his fair locks. The bleeding Elijah stumbled over to his friends and collapsed next to them.

"Who the hell are you to interfere here?" the sheriff asked, directing his question at Major Frost, who had dismounted and was approaching him. "This boy is my prisoner. He has murdered a man out at Jericho Plantation and looks like he has done killed two more here."

The major removed his gloves and bent down next to Isaac to check on him. Recognition came to the boy immediately.

"M-Major Frost...I-I knew you'd come," Isaac managed to say, holding his hand up to him.

The major placed a comforting hand on the boy's shoulder.

"It's all right now, son. It's all over. Try not to talk. We'll get you up to the fort and the doctor will have a good look at you."

"He'll do nothing of the kind!" the sheriff exclaimed. "This is a civil matter, not a military one! I'm taking that boy with me. He's a murderer and I aim tuh bring him tuh justice at the end of a rope!"

The major stood up wearing a slight grin.

"Wrong, Sheriff. First, you have no jurisdiction here. You are standing on federal property. Second, the boy is a hero, not a murderer. Third, if you try to take him, I'll personally plant you six feet under the ground without the slightest hesitation!"

He turned to the rest of the posse, who were still mounted and watching to see what was going to transpire. "That goes for the rest of you. I'll give you a minute to ride out of here or suffer the consequences."

"Ah have got a warrant right here in muh pocket," the sheriff said, pulling out the paper from his jacket. "Signed by Judge Britton!"

"That warrant has been rescinded. The judge's son, Walter, convinced him it was a bogus charge. He investigated that supposed murder and uncovered a whole lot of incriminating evidence against the Jerichos who were plotting to murder Isaac Barker after forging their uncle's will in their favor."

"That's a lie!" Joseph screamed standing up and advancing toward the major. "What evidence do you have?"

The major pointed to the saddlebag on his horse.

"Walter Britton was given a journal by Mrs. Jericho. She also gave him other papers and correspondence written by Charles Braxton that state the plan in great detail. I doubt she knew what was in the journal or what the papers were, but Mr. Britton is a thorough investigator. Apparently, Braxton poisoned Isaac's uncle, who was his guardian. He used the boy as a convenient excuse to come to Virginia to remove himself as a possible suspect if the old man's death was investigated. I can assure you, Sheriff, that when I return to Boston there will be a thorough investigation and an autopsy performed to see if the body contains any arsenic."

Joseph's face became ashen, and he backed up toward his horse. "Lies! All lies!" he declared, mounting his horse, and taking a last look at his dead father. He then rode off, followed by Carl and the rest of his sycophantic cronies.

The major merely watched them go. There was plenty of time to deal with them later.

"That boy still murdered Braxton, regardless of what he might have done!" the sheriff exclaimed.

"Wrong again," Major Frost said, lighting a cigarette and blowing a few puffy circles into the cold morning air. "According to the butler, Lucias, who witnessed the whole thing, Charles Braxton dragged the young girl, Joy, from the house to the stable with the intention of whipping her, all because she burned his toast. Young Isaac here, who is as gallant as they come, attempted to stop him and indeed was successful in his endeavor. A scuffle ensued after Braxton attacked the boy. He was merely defending himself. As far as these two dead scoundrels lying here in the grass, they received their just rewards by attempting to assault the boy. I do believe that if you ask the sentry standing up there on the palisade, he will reaffirm what I have just told you. But it matters not, Sheriff. The boy is coming with me and that is the end of it."

The sheriff's face turned hard. He was still holding his cudgel as if he wanted to brain Isaac with it, but instead pointed it at Joy who was examining Isaac's head, which she determined was not a serious injury.

"She is the property of Joseph Jericho. Ah will be taking her with me," the sheriff said.

He went to grab her wrist but before he could reach it, Isaac pushed Joy away and stood between her and the sheriff, waving his blade. "You'll not take her anywhere. She's a human being. She belongs to no one but herself."

Major Frost intervened, stepping next to Isaac and gently lowered his arm which was holding the extended blade. "Sheriff, if I were you, I would mount that horse of yours and count your blessings."

For a few seconds the big man stood his ground, but after assessing the situation and realizing the odds were against him, he stormed off with a flurry of curses. "You've not heard the last of me, Major Frost!"

Isaac glanced at the dead body of Wil Jericho. Elijah was kneeling next to his father's corpse and looked up at Isaac and Joy as they approached him.

"Shouldn't I be feelin' sad or somethin'?"

They knelt next to him, and the three youths embraced and that is when Elijah was overcome with grief, not for the death of his father but for the father he never had.

Chapter 21

J oy awoke at the crack of dawn with one of her headaches that was so debilitating she feared her head might explode. She had been given a small bunk in a separate room in the fort, isolated from the barracks where all the men slept, including Isaac and Elijah. She sat up.

It was still dark, and she felt for the pitcher of water on the table next to her bunk. She could see nothing except whirling circles that seemed to fly in and out of her range of vision. Her small fingers finally found the pitcher, but she did not even have the strength to pick it up. She fell back onto her pillow and weakly massaged her temples. Finally, mercifully, the headache began to subside, and her vision returned, albeit slowly.

The headaches were becoming more frequent, and she feared one of these days she would not be able to recover as quickly. She poured some water into the tin cup she had been provided with and sipped on it, letting it soothe her parched throat.

Peering out the small window she could see the first rays of light on the horizon and smiled. She felt blessed. Life had been hard for her, but she realized it was hard for a lot of people and for the first time she concluded that not all people were bad. She thought about Moses. He had been the only one who had ever been kind to her, except for Elijah, who did not have a mean bone in his body and, sometimes, Mother Etta. Otherwise, people had treated her roughly and with a great deal of condescension. Then she thought about her sister, Esther. She had almost forgotten about her. It had seemed like ages since she had seen her. She missed her and longed to see her again.

She wondered what it would be like in Massachusetts. She had read about the history of the American Revolution and all she could think about was Bunker Hill. Perhaps Isaac could show her the place? But it was Bandy's pond she really looked forward to seeing, and of course, Bandy himself.

She often wondered if it was true. Did Bandy really talk to Isaac? She talked to the animals, but did Pink, her rabbit, really talk back to her? Or had it all been in her mind? She was now convinced it was the latter. She had talked to Pink out of sheer loneliness, and it made her feel better to believe Pink was talking back to her. Perhaps this was Isaac's way of dealing with loneliness also? She pondered the possibilities. The two of them were so much alike in that sense.

A noise from outside broke her from her reveries and, wiping the condensation from the window, she noticed a rank of soldiers standing at attention, their muskets at order arms. Major Frost was walking up the line with his sergeant inspecting the men's uniforms and checking to see if their brass was polished to a shine. She stood up and threw on her cloak.

It was bitterly cold outside and the heat from the small hearth in the adjacent room hardly lessened the chill. She had just finished making her bed when she heard footsteps in the hallway outside her door. Then, a light tap. She opened it to find a smiling Isaac standing there. He was decked out in a blue military uniform, replete with polished buttons and brass. He was wearing a new pair of brogans and a starched kepi on his head.

"How do you like it, Joy? The major has given me the honorary rank of corporal. Since I can play the bugle, he has made me a bugle boy until the *Pegasus* leaves. Did you hear reveille this morning? That was me! The regular bugler has taken ill, so I am filling in for him. The major told me when I finish school, he can get me an appointment at West Point!" he said. "That's a few years away, though."

She hugged him and they sat down next to each other on her bunk. "Isaac?"

He was looking at her warmly. "Yeah?"

"Tell me more about Bandy. I...I had a dream last night. I was with you, and we were at a lake. The buds were on the trees, and suddenly, the whole sky was filled with pigeons! And we were dancing! You were playing your harmonica, and I was singing. And the birds, they seemed to be singing with us!"

Isaac's face brightened. With all that had gone on over the past few days he had almost forgotten about Bandy. It seemed like so long ago, almost as if he had been a different person.

"Joy, when we arrive in Massachusetts you will see your sister and meet my little brother, Thomas. He is a talker and asks tons of questions. He's a pain sometimes, but he's my little brother and I love him. We have a great big carriage and a driver. He can take us to the lake, and you can meet Bandy and even speak to him! He will love you, Joy!"

She looked down at her feet and was playing with one of the buttons on her cloak. "Isaac...are you sure Bandy can speak? I mean, I talk to the animals, too, and...and I think my bunny, Pink, talks," she said, "but...but now I am not sure."

The boy became quiet, and she was worried that she might have hurt his feelings. "You...you don't believe me, Joy?"

She smiled. "Of course, I believe you, Isaac. I'm just asking that's all. I...I want to see Bandy and all the wonderful things at the lake. It seems like a magical place, and I can't wait to see it!"

He placed his hand on top of hers. "Well, Joy. You are going to see it and many more delightful things. We live in a big house! It's not as big as Jericho Plantation but it is stately enough. Although I will have to figure out how to run it. Since Uncle Raymond is dead, it will be up to me, but there is a lawyer that knows all of Uncle's finances and I am sure he will help me through it."

She glanced out the window at the ranks of soldiers. Major Frost was inspecting a musket. "It all seems like a dream, Isaac. Does it not?" she asked, turning to him.

He nodded. "The last few weeks have certainly seemed like a dream. But something good has come out of it, Joy. We never would have met and become best friends if none of it happened."

There was a shuffling sound outside in the hallway and a young private appeared in the doorway. "Corporal Barker, the major sent me to fetch you. He wants to see you in his office."

Isaac smiled at Joy and left her sitting on the bed staring out the window. Major Frost was gone, and the sergeant was drilling the men. She watched the pivoting movements and disciplined ranks with amazement. It was so regimented and orderly. Isaac would make a good soldier, she thought.

****

Isaac found the major smoking a pipe shuffling through a folder of papers on his desk. He looked up when Isaac snapped to attention in front of his desk.

"Ah! You are a natural-born soldier, Isaac... or I should say, Corporal Barker."

"Yes, sir. One day I should like to be an officer in the army, and I am looking forward to the day when I am commissioned."

The good major smiled and told Isaac to have a seat. "I have some good news for you...and, well, some bad, too. The *Pegasus* leaves at 0800 in the morning and you and I will be on it. I have been given leave to accompany you to Boston. Captain Rogers will take charge of the fort. Somehow your case has attracted unwanted attention with the pro-slavery folks who want to see you hang and the girl, Joy, returned to Jericho Plantation. Of course, the murder charge has been dropped. All the evidence is in your favor, thanks to the detective work of Walter Britton, who, speaking of the devil, now stands in the doorway behind you."

Isaac turned to see the man whom he had unhorsed a few days earlier leaning on his crutches, his broken leg in a plaster cast.

"Well, Corporal Barker, are yuh gonna help me sit down or are yuh gonna let me stand here grinnin' in the doorway?"

Isaac smiled, surprised to see the man he and Joy had left in the woods near the railroad tracks a few days before. "Yes, sir!" Isaac exclaimed, pulling over a chair from the wall and helping his former adversary sit down.

Isaac held out his hand and the judge's son clasped it firmly.

"Sir, I want to thank you for all that you have done helping me and Joy. I am indebted to you, good sir, and I hope there are no hard feelings for the fact that I am responsible for breaking your leg. Had I known what type of man you were, I never would have fired that derringer."

Walter studied the boy with a twinkle in his eye. "Well, Corporal, I am sure glad yuh did fire that pistol, as we shouldn't be here talking like this if yuh hadn't. Also, don't you worry none about muh old leg. I deserved what I got, for I was in the wrong. As far as being indebted to me, think nothin' of it. If anything, I am indebted to you and Joy for letting me see the light."

"Well said," Major Frost declared, sitting back in his chair blowing circles with his pipe. "Now, to get to the crux of the matter, Mr. Britton, I was just telling Corporal Barker about our departure on board the *Pegasus* tomorrow morning. I have already informed Captain Mayberry about the situation and that there may be trouble. Joseph Jericho has sworn vengeance. However, once young Barker here is safely aboard, and a strong guard posted on the quay in front of the vessel, he will be beyond their reach."

Walter was tapping one of his crutches with his stubby fingers and then raised a finger. "This sheriff seems to be in the Jerichos pocket. I have heard talk he is gonna have warrants signed by a pro-slavery judge for the re-arrest of young Barker. He will also have warrants for the arrests of Joy and Elijah Jericho for aiding and abetting a fugitive. We need to consider this, as once they leave the safety of the fort, they will be considered fair game under Virginia law."

Isaac was chewing on his lower lip. He had not even thought about this possibility, but his good friend the major had it all figured out for him.

"I have considered this, Mr. Britton," the major said, with his pipe held between his thumb and forefinger. "As you well know, young Barker here is now a corporal in the United States army, though only on a ten-day enlistment. As such, he is subject to the Articles of War and military justice. A simple order of arrest, signed by me, will put him beyond the reach of the civil authorities of Virginia. Of course, once the *Pegasus* is put to sea, the warrant shall be ripped to shreds and its fragments scattered in Chesapeake Bay. It is a mere formality. The same shall be done for Private Elijah Jericho, who will also be accompanying us."

Isaac leaned forward in his chair. "Sir, what about Joy? How will we get her on board?"

"That is going to be the tricky part, Corporal Barker. Obviously, she cannot enlist in the United States Army. Though, no doubt, I believe she would make a great nurse. Therefore, we will have to secret her out tonight in a wagon under a strong guard."

Isaac seemed to contemplate this.

"Sir, I request permission to accompany, Joy," Isaac said.

Major Frost blew a few rings from his pipe and clasped his hands behind his head.

"As her champion, I knew that you would ask this," he said. "But it is totally out of the question. Your presence with the guard would draw immediate suspicion that something of the sort was afoot. Joy will have to be packaged among the straw and crates on the wagon, as if she were a commodity going to market rather than a human being. Remember, even though this is military business, the wagon is still subject to be searched by custom agents on the dock. Joy must be hidden until the *Pegasus* is put to sea. Only then will she be out of reach of Virginia authorities. I know this is not what you wanted to hear, but unfortunately, it is what we must do."

Isaac stood up and nervously shoved his hands into the pockets of his trousers. "Sir, what if they do a search of the wagon and find her? What then? Surely, we would not give her up?"

"We will deal with that when the situation arises," Major Frost said calmly. "Captain Rogers will be in charge of this nocturnal mission, and he is a top-rate officer. I have told him to use his discretion but by no means is Joy to be turned over to Virginia authorities. Tensions between the states and the federal government are near a boiling point due to the election of Lincoln. We must hope this little disagreement does not provoke an incident that will create a spark. Do you understand my meaning, Corporal Barker?"

Isaac sat back down in his chair. "Yes, sir, I do. And I trust your judgement implicitly. It's just the thought of being here doing nothing will cause me great anxiety."

The major nodded. "And that is totally understandable. But you must have patience. It will work out well in the end. Now, we must prepare Joy for this ordeal and the risks that go with it. I leave that in your capable hands."

Isaac thanked the major and Walter and took his leave. He found Joy talking with Elijah, who was also dressed in the uniform of a regular.

"Hey, cousin," Elijah said with a smirk. "How come ah'm only a private? Does that mean ah have tuh take orders from yuh?"

Isaac clapped his cousin on the back. "What do you think, Joy? Should I take Cousin Elijah outside and make him drill until he drops?"

Joy placed a finger on her chin and winked at Elijah. "I don't know, Isaac. I think Elijah has had too much excitement, but a little drill might not hurt him."

Elijah chuckled. "On a serious note, what did the major tell yuh?"

"That's what we need to talk about," Isaac replied.

He filled Joy and Elijah in on the details, including Joy being secreted away in the dead of night. She was understandably apprehensive, but immediately agreed to the adventure. Until then, they spent their time walking around the courtyard. Isaac and Elijah even received some one-on-one musket training with the sergeant, a rough-looking Irishman named O'Rourke. The two boys quickly caught on and were apt pupils, which impressed the sergeant greatly.

It seemed forever, but eventually darkness once again set over the fort and Isaac took his bugle and played "Taps."

Joy was to leave at 0500. To make it look like legitimate business, the wagon was packed with crates and a couple of small four-pounder cannons. One of the crates was equipped with a false bottom lined with a blanket and some straw to make Joy's ride to the *Pegasus* as comfortable as possible. She was also given a canteen of water and some biscuits in case she had to spend a considerable time in the crate. However, Major Frost estimated the trip would take less than an hour. Once on board the *Pegasus*, the crate would be taken to Isaac's cabin and opened when Isaac and the major were safely on board the ship.

When the time came, Joy was ready, and bravely climbed into the crate without the slightest hesitation. It was a small crate, but Joy was a small girl and she easily nestled down into the blanket and straw. Isaac handed her the canteen and biscuits. He swallowed hard, his brow wrinkled in concern.

"Joy, we...we will be following you within the hour," he said nervously.

She knew the risks, but her courage was unshaken. She winked at the boy who was more anxious at the thought of her spending an hour or two confined in a crate than she was.

"Don't worry about me, Isaac. You take care of yourself. I will be fine," she said, attempting to assuage his apprehension for her wellbeing.

They clasped hands and it was all he could do to pull his hand away from hers. They had been through so much together over the last few days that it was now hard to separate. Isaac watched as the false bottom was anchored in place using strong oak dowels. The rest of the crate was filled with straw and some stirrups and other saddle equipment. This was a precautionary measure in case someone was to open it. The wagon was to be escorted by Captain Rogers and a troop of cavalry, twelve strong. Major Frost and a small contingent of men, along with Isaac and Elijah, would follow an hour later.

Isaac watched with a lump in his throat as Captain Rogers and the wagon departed through the main gate, guided only by the morning moonlight.

Chapter 22

Joy felt the rumble-tumble of the pot-holed road leading into Norfolk proper. She could hear one of the soldiers whistling a tune and began humming it to herself. She was not in the least bit nervous, though she could not help but feel a little anxious at the thought of Isaac following in her wake. Until they were all safely on board the *Pegasus* there was still a risk.

It was hard for her to estimate the amount of time that had elapsed since the wagon had started out, but she estimated at least twenty minutes had gone by when she heard the deep voice of Captain Rogers issue a command to halt. The wagon came to a stop, and she could hear the low voices of a couple of the soldiers, but they were too far away for her to discern what they were saying.

Joy tried not to move inside the crate. For all she knew, there was someone standing next to the wagon listening. She wondered what the holdup was as she was certain they had not yet reached the *Pegasus*. After a few dreadful minutes of waiting, she heard the snorting nostrils and pounding hooves of many horses and then a voice, asking for the whereabouts of Isaac Barker. She recognized it as the nasally twang of Sheriff Connors.

"Isaac Barker is not among us," Captain Rogers said, "but even if he was, we would not be obligated to turn him over to you, partner."

"You are no longer protected by the confines of the fort, Cap'n. How do ah know yuh ain't got him hidden thar among this cargo?" Sheriff Connors replied.

Joy heard something shuffling around in the back of the wagon. Whatever it was, it was really close to her, and she suddenly felt a sick feeling in her gut.

"Sheriff, order that fella down off that wagon!" the captain hollered. "Yuh have no warrant, nor are yuh a custom officer."

"I don't need a warrant, Cap'n. You're within the city of Norfolk, Virginia. This is my city and I got probable cause to believe a fugitive from justice is among your cargo."

Joy did not know it, but the sheriff had gathered all his deputies and a small army of volunteers, nearing fifty men, including Joseph Jericho and Carl. He had concealed them along the road and when the small contingent of men under Captain Rogers appeared, they broke out of the tree line and surrounded the soldiers who were outnumbered four to one.

What the sheriff did not know, however, was that the canny and shrewd captain had left two of his men to follow at a distance in case something like this happened. Mounted on two of the fastest horses in the stable, they turned and headed back to the fort as fast as they could for reinforcements.

Major Frost was just saddling his horse when the two messengers arrived, their mounts wet from their exertion told the major and Isaac, who was standing nearby, that something had gone wrong.

"Sir, there is a strong party of men surrounding the wagon, at least two score, maybe more. I'm not sure what their motives are, as we were well back from them."

The major appeared grave but was cool and calm delivering his orders.

"There will be a fight. They are no match for disciplined troops, but we must hurry! Tell the men to forget any unnecessary accoutrements and prepare for a hard ride."

Isaac grabbed the major's sleeve. "Sir, it is me they are after, but if they find Joy, they might as well have me, too!"

The good major shook his head. "They will have no one if I have anything to say about it. I'm going to head out with two dozen men, and you and Elijah can follow in the wagon with Sergeant O'Rourke and three or four others."

Isaac started to protest but realized the futility of it. He was no horseman and would only slow the rest of the party down if he were to saddle one and ride out with them. The major and his party would get there in no time, assess the situation, and perhaps have it in hand by the time he arrived with Elijah and Sergeant O'Rourke.

He sprinted into the barracks and grabbed Elijah who was packing his bag of meagre essentials that the army had provided him into a duffel bag. Isaac had already packed his and, after explaining the new developments to his cousin, they raced out into the courtyard to find Sergeant O'Rourke hitching up the team. The major and his band of disciplined cavalry had already left.

"We are taking two privates with us, Corporal Barker," the sergeant said gruffly. "See to it while I finish with the wagon."

"Yes, sergeant."

Isaac hurried back into the barracks. Most of the men were still sleeping as it was early and reveille was still nearly an hour away. He found four men on duty in the common room sitting around a table playing a game of poker.

"I need two volunteers," Isaac said.

The four men were all staring at him as if he had lost his mind.

"For what? We are getting ready to be off duty thar, Corporal."

Isaac shuffled uneasily. "We are going to see some action on the road to Norfolk. The civil authorities have surrounded our wagon. Major Frost has already left, and Sergeant O'Rourke sent me to fetch two of you to accompany us."

"Well, why didn't yuh say so, Corporal? Come on fellas!" said a big-boned man, throwing his cards down on the table. "Let's help the little corporal out!"

The men quickly donned their sack coats and kepis and grabbed their muskets. Isaac suddenly realized he had four volunteers wanting to see a little action. He would be hard pressed to get two of them to stand down, but he managed it, choosing the big-boned private whose name was Garret and a young sturdy fellow from Mississippi who went by the name of Skeeter. They climbed on back of the wagon and sat down among some empty crates next to Elijah who was carefully inspecting his pistol. Isaac sat down on the spring seat next to Sergeant O'Rourke, who had taken the reins and set the wagon in motion.

"You men back there have your muskets loaded," the sergeant said, cocking a thumb at them. "Things might get a little hot here in a few minutes."

Isaac checked his Colt and stuffed it back into its holster.

"Don't yuh worry none, young'un," Sergeant O'Rourke said, coughing into his hand. "Major Frost is one fella that doesn't take kindly tuh this sort o' thing."

"Well, I certainly hope he gets there in time," Isaac replied. "From what that messenger said, there are at least forty or fifty of them surrounding the wagon."

"Fifty bumpkins," the sergeant said scornfully. "They won't stand no chance against regulars."

Isaac hoped the sergeant was right, but inwardly felt anxiety over Joy's situation. He felt the breeze on his cheeks and glanced back at Elijah who was in deep conversation with Garret and Skeeter. Isaac could hear the Mississippian attempting to impress Elijah with tales of manly, heroic feats. Skeeter's wild tall tales were suddenly interrupted by the sound of distant gunfire. At first, only a single shot. However, this was quickly followed by a rapid volley of numerous shots that echoed ominously into the cool morning darkness.

"Looks like things are heatin' up, boys!" the sergeant bellowed. "Use them crates and gunny sacks for cover and get ready to blaze away when I tell yuh!"

Surprisingly, Isaac did not feel the least amount of fear, though the same could not be said for Elijah. He nervously pulled out his Colt and squatted behind a crate next to Skeeter. Elijah was trembling but put a bold face on it and tried not to show his fear. He was determined to fight bravely despite his anxiety.

The sergeant ordered Isaac to take a position next to Garret, which he reluctantly did, preferring to stay seated on the spring seat next to the sergeant where he could get a better look at what was going on. However, he acquiesced to the sergeant's prudent order, realizing that with bullets flying everywhere, it would be far safer for him to be among the crates.

The next few minutes seemed like an eternity for Isaac. Every now and then he would lift his head up over the buckboard to see if he could see anything and finally Garret yanked him back down.

"Dang it, boy, I know that you are a corporal and me just a lowly old private but yer gonna get yer head shot off unnecessarily. Now, stay down, blast it!"

Isaac swallowed hard and listened as the sound of gunfire continued, getting louder as they got nearer. Turning a bend in the road, they ran right into the middle of a score of fleeing horses, some of them without riders, coming from the direction of the gunshots. Isaac recognized the stalwart form of Joseph Jericho among the throng. They paid no attention to the wagon, and it was obvious they had been routed by the arrival of Major Frost and his band of cavalry.

They arrived to find the major talking with Captain Rogers. Joy had been released from her crate and was tending to one of the soldiers who had sustained a grazing gunshot wound to his leg.

Isaac scanned the area around the wagon and could see five bodies, all members of Joseph Jericho's mercenary mob. One of them was still alive. Isaac immediately recognized him as the lubberly Carl who had been shot in the gut. He was groaning miserably in a pool of blood, begging for someone to bring him water. Elijah obliged, holding his canteen up to his lips. The stricken man gulped down the water, letting it drool down onto his beard.

"Traitor!" he exclaimed painfully, managing to point a stubby finger at the boy before regurgitating blood and expiring.

Elijah ignored him and returned to where Joy was tending to the soldier's leg. She had sent Isaac to get some cloth while she bathed the wound with water. When Isaac returned, she bound the leg with the cloth, and they helped the injured man onto the back of the wagon.

"They won't be tryin' anything else like that anytime soon. I can assure you that!" Captain Rogers exclaimed.

The major lit his pipe and approached Sheriff Connors.

"You can ride on out of here, Sheriff," the major said. "Next time you bring a mob to attack United States Regulars you had better think twice."

"You haven't heard the last of me thar, Major Frost. Those men were deputized, and ah will have yuh charged with murdering lawmen!"

"Do your best, Sheriff. According to my captain here, your men attacked us with no provocation. As far as being deputized, that doesn't give them the right to attack federal troops who are performing legitimate business."

The sheriff was red in the face and started to say something but thought better of it and stormed off toward his horse. He passed Isaac along the way, the boy giving him a reproachful look.

"Yuh lucky thar, Yankee boy. Let me get another chance and ah will have yuh swingin' from the gallows!"

Isaac brushed him off. The sheriff would never get another chance, as far as he was concerned. He would soon be on the *Pegasus.* He watched the beaten man mount his horse and ride off in the direction of the ferry. Isaac wondered if he might try to make another attempt with Joseph Jericho to capture them. He doubted it. They had been thoroughly whipped and if they did come back for a second round, it wouldn't be on this night and by tomorrow he and Joy would be long gone.

Major Frost ordered Captain Rogers and his contingent of men to load the bodies of Carl and the others onto the wagon that had previously carried Joy. They would then return to the fort and attempt to discern who they were so that their families could be notified to claim them.

He decided it was now safe to proceed with only a small escort to the *Pegasus*. No longer was Joy forced to ride in a crate. The danger had passed. Major Frost had done all that he could have to avoid a confrontation with the civil authorities. The sheriff and Joseph Jericho had played their hand and had been repulsed. Hopefully, the incident would be downplayed and not become a rallying cry for the secessionists, who were suspicious of any sort of federal interference. If it did, so be it. The major concluded he had not been the aggressor and therefore was only protecting the interests of his command. He had been set on and attacked by what he considered an organized rabble and lynch mob. That is how he intended on writing up the report.

Isaac, Joy, and Elijah climbed back onto the wagon with Garret and Skeeter while the major kept a dozen mounted men to act as their escort. They would be posted in a defensive position on the quay in front of the *Pegasus* until that vessel was under way. He was taking no chances.

The streets of Norfolk were almost deserted as dawn was just breaking and it would be an hour or two before the citizenry would come to life, not realizing a small battle had taken place just north of the city. They passed the hotel where Isaac had spent the first night on his arrival. It seemed like ages ago, yet only a week had passed. It wasn't long before the familiar shape of the *Pegasus* took form, its boilers already lit and ready to go.

Captain Mayberry met them on the quay. He had heard all about Isaac's trials and tribulations and had even considered coming inland to help find the boy. In the end, however, he figured his duty was to get the *Pegasus* ready to steam out on the day Isaac arrived. He had never held up a departure for one person, but he was willing to make an exception in this case, even if he should have to wait a few weeks to do so. He had taken a liking to the boy and being an ardent abolitionist himself, he could think of no other way to help the cause than shuttle Isaac and Joy away from the peril of the Virginia authorities.

Once Major Frost had posted the guard, he boarded the *Pegasus*, followed by Isaac, Joy, and Elijah. Once on board, Elijah approached Isaac and held out his hand. He was glum and Isaac could read the conflict of emotions on his face.

"I guess this is where we depart, cousin," Elijah said.

"Depart?" Isaac was confused, but mechanically held out his hand.

"Ah guess ah will go back tuh the big house and take muh licks. Ah got nowhere tuh go up in Boston."

Isaac shook his head. "No, sir, that's where you are wrong, Cousin Elijah. You're coming with us. Isn't that right, Joy?"

Joy was listening to the two boys talk and stepped forward, looking up at Elijah. "You can't return home, Elijah. Your brother will kill you! He hates you as much as he does Isaac."

Elijah frowned and scratched the back of his head. "But I ain't got any money or nothing. What would I do?"

Isaac placed a hand on his cousin's shoulder. He was grinning. "Money? By God, cousin, Uncle Raymond just left us a fortune!"

"He left you a fortune, not me, Isaac. And yuh deserve it. The Jericho's are bad people, and ah am a Jericho. Or did yuh forget?"

"Uncle Raymond was your uncle, too," Isaac said. "Or did you forget? As far as I am concerned, there is enough money for all of us and I'll not hear another word about it. You are coming with us, Elijah, and that's that!"

Joy reached out and hugged the confused boy. "Just because you are a Jericho doesn't mean you are bad," she said in a firm but caring tone. "I bet there are people in my family that are bad, too. There are bad people and good people, Elijah, and it doesn't matter what your name is. I know one thing: You are a good person."

He was overcome with emotion, and Joy saw a tear fall down his cheek.

"Okay, I reckon ah will come along," he finally said, wiping the tears away. "But just kick my darn butt overboard if ah git in the way."

The three youths laughed and embraced.

Captain Mayberry was anxious to get away, fearing some trouble might come, but Major Frost assured him all was well. The *Pegasus* was set to depart at 0800.

It was shortly before the gangway was removed, and all passengers had boarded, that an elderly man in a dark suit, wearing a black beaver hat, pulled down low, stepped onto the ramp. He was accompanied by a stout gentleman with a red handlebar moustache and bushy sideburns, who asked to speak with the captain. After a short conversation, Captain Mayberry called over Major Frost and the three men had a reserved conversation before the major finally approached the three youths.

"Well, it appears we have lost one of the first-class cabins," he said glumly. "I just gave mine up to that old gentleman wearing the beaver."

"Dang it, sir," Elijah said, stuffing his cold hands in his pockets. "If I didn't know no better, that old fella looks just like President Buchanan."

The major grinned. "Private Jericho, you are an astute observer of men, as that is exactly who he is."

Isaac's mouth dropped and he looked at Joy who was similarly starstruck and rendered speechless.

"Well, ah'll be!" Elijah exclaimed. "I wonder if he remembers me? I think I'll go ask him."

He started to walk toward the president, but the major pulled him back.

"Let's be discreet and give the president a little privacy, shall we?"

"Yes, sir," Elijah responded, disappointed at the lost chance of talking the president's ear off.

"I am going to bunk in the captain's quarters," the major said. "Joy will take the other cabin. Since girls and boys cannot share cabins, you

two boys will have to make do out here on the
deck the best you can. If it rains you can go below
and join the passengers in steerage or take cover
under one of the stairwells. I'll see if I can round up
a few blankets."

"Yes, sir. We can tough it out, sir," Isaac said
cheerfully, throwing his arm around his cousin's
shoulder. "All that has happened over the past
week has hardened me to anything. I'll be in
heaven sleeping under that stairwell tonight. What
says you, cousin?"

Elijah nodded, twisting his mouth in an
exaggerated way. "Ah second what muh cousin just
said, but ah will add that ah will probably spend
most of the time leanin' ovuh that rail emptyin' the
contents of muh stomach intuh the sea. Ah don't
do well on boats, if yuh know what I mean!"

Everyone laughed except Joy, who offered
Elijah her bed if he got too ill. However, the boy
declined, not wanting to look unchivalrous.

It wasn't long before the *Pegasus* was put
to sea. Their first port of call was Ocean City, on the
Maryland coast. By the time they arrived, Elijah had
emptied his breakfast into the Atlantic Ocean. Joy
and Isaac had set him on a blanket on the deck and
attempted to do what they could for him, which
wasn't much. Elijah's face was ashen. Joy, too, had

one of her spells, which were becoming more frequent, but she quickly recovered as if nothing had happened and attended to Elijah's suffering.

There was a delay at Ocean City that ran into the late afternoon. One of the boilers had broken down. Isaac could hear Captain Mayberry cussing at the mechanic as they attempted to repair the valve on one of the injectors. They finished just before dusk and once again *Pegasus* was put to sea, much to Elijah's displeasure. The boy, sick as he was, still refused to take Joy's bed. It was just after dark when Joy and Isaac, who were squatting down attending to Elijah's sickness, felt the presence of someone lurking behind them. They looked up at the same time to see the stooped-over form of President Buchanan hovering over them.

Isaac immediately stood up and popped to attention, saluting the president, who made a half-hearted effort to salute the boy in return.

"At ease, young man. I see that my disguise with this beaver hat is a rather feeble effort," the president said with a wink.

"Oh no, sir," Isaac replied nervously. "It's just that my cousin Elijah here recognized you when you came aboard, that's all. Though, I must say, sir, that I probably would have recognized you from seeing your likeness in the newspapers."

"You have proven my point, corporal," the president said stuffing his hands in the pockets of his long cloak. "You are young for a soldier. What is your name? Are you a drummer boy or a bugler?"

"Corporal Isaac Barker, sir. I am a bugler, but only enlisted for ten days. This is Joy and my cousin, Elijah Jericho, who as you can well see, is sort of indisposed at the moment."

The president chuckled. "I can see that plainly, Corporal Barker. My guard, Langley, has also taken ill in these rough seas. Now, listen to me, I want you to take this sick boy up to my cabin and give him my bunk. It won't do to have him out here to catch a chill. Do you hear?"

Elijah protested and started to rise, but immediately leaned over the rail and dry heaved into the sea. "I-I'm b-better, sir. I can tough it out," Elijah said feebly. Isaac and Joy had each grabbed one of his arms to help him stand.

"That's not a request, young man; that's an order," President Buchanan said with a quick nod of his head, his eyes blinking rapidly. "Now, see to it."

Elijah was quick to agree with the president. He secretly was extremely glad it was an order. It wasn't long before he was hustled away into the president's berth and was soon wrapped comfortably in his wool blanket. Langley moaned in his sufferings on the top bunk, and Joy went to work and did her best to relieve his sickness, for which he was quite grateful. Isaac and President Buchanan hovered over the grate in the floor letting the heat warm them. The seas had become turbulent, and it became obvious a storm was approaching.

Major Frost, when he found out President Buchanan had given Elijah his bunk, offered the president his own berth in the captain's cabin, which was nothing more than a pile of warm blankets on the deck. The president, however, refused his offer but did retire to the captain's cabin for a cup of hot chocolate, insisting that Isaac and Joy join him.

Captain Mayberry was busy below deck attempting to sort out another issue with one of the boilers. The quartet, including the president, sat around the captain's table chatting about the weather when the president turned to Joy, who had thus far remained silent.

"Young lady, I see you seem to have a way with healing the sick. Where did you learn your profession? I take it you are free and not enslaved?"

Joy took a sip of her hot chocolate feeling the warmth from the tin mug in her hands.

"I learned to heal from my older sister, Esther. And yes, sir, I am now free. Thanks to Isaac here and Major Frost. It did not come easy, but I must say my faith in humanity has been restored somewhat."

The president cocked an eyebrow. "That is splendid, young Joy. And it is good to know that you have been released from the bondage of slavery. If you hadn't been, I should have bought your freedom myself, a practice which I have done before. Slavery is a vile institution and a blight on humanity. The sooner it is extinguished from the earth, the better off we all shall be."

"Hear! Hear! Sir, well said!" Isaac exclaimed, raising his mug in salute, to which the president replied by raising his and clinking them together.

The vibrant and cheerful tone of the president, however, was short-lived. He seemed to become distracted by something whirling around in his head and when he spoke again it was in a melancholic and reserved tone.

"These are trying times," he said quietly. "I wish the incoming president the best of luck, but I believe we are on the verge of something that has been festering in this country since its separation from the mother country in the last century. I...I only wish I could have done more to prevent it."

He lowered his head and when he raised it again, Isaac and Joy could have sworn they saw a tear run down his old, wrinkled cheek. The girl, sympathetic to the old man, reached over and touched his hand, a simple gesture that reached to the soul of the man, who for the first time since they had become acquainted, managed to smile.

Chapter 23

The carriage waiting on them at the train station in Boston had been arranged by telegraph by Major Frost. He had contacted Isaac's attorney, Robert Metcalf, who was patiently waiting for them on the platform. Robert was a dapper-looking gentleman wearing a tweed coat. He sported a thick, neatly trimmed blond beard and mustache. To Isaac, he looked quite the dandy. He greeted them cordially with a large, outstretched hand that seemed to swallow Isaac's with his firm grip.

"Young Barker, I first want to tell you how sorry I am regarding your great-uncle. He was a fine man," Robert said with genuine sorrow. "The investigation is continuing but the coroner has found definite signs of arsenic in his body. There is no doubt he was murdered by that villain."

Isaac swallowed. "Thank you, sir. I must admit I am quite overwhelmed by everything that has happened."

Robert was rubbing his beard. "You have no reason to worry in that regard. The estate has been left in a trust under my care until you reach your majority. Your uncle's shipping company is being run by a competent colleague of his. You shall meet him in due time. He will fill you in on the particulars of running a business and you shall spend summers under his guidance after your school year has ended."

"Yes, sir," Isaac replied. "But I plan on going to West Point."

"That can be arranged with the major here, who has agreed to act as your guardian, as well as your brother's and, of course, Joy's, also."

Major Frost was smiling and when he held out his hand, Isaac grasped it. Then, quite overcome by joyous sentiment and reacting to his sudden good fortune, he hugged the man.

"I...I don't know what to say," Isaac said. "You have been too kind, sir."

"Well, Corporal Barker, let us go see your brother and Joy's sister. I imagine they are quite anxious to see you," the major said, slightly embarrassed by the boy's public display of affection, especially since they were in uniform.

They entered the carriage, the three youths sitting across from the lawyer and the major. It was snowing hard when they arrived at the gate to the Barker mansion. A new butler was there waiting for them to arrive. A pleasant-looking man with porkchop sideburns and a ruddy face. A big difference from the irascible, Charles.

Isaac and Joy could see their siblings standing under the portico. Thomas, dressed in a fine suit, no longer able to suppress his excitement, ran out into the snow, waving his little arms at the carriage. When it came to a gravelly halt, Isaac leaped out, scooped his younger brother up into the air and twirled him around as if he were a toy before showering him with kisses and hugs.

"Isaac! Isaac! I thought you would never come back!" the younger boy screamed into the wintery mist, tears in his eyes. "I'm so happy!"

Joy rushed to meet her sister. She barely recognized her, as it had been two years since they had last seen one another, and both girls had grown taller. Esther, however, was horrified by Joy's gaunt appearance, though she tried not to show it.

The major and the lawyer followed the youths inside. The new manservant, whose name was Redding, started a rip-roaring fire. Since it was almost supper time, the dining room had been set up by Mary, Uncle Raymond's old maid, and the food prepared by Emilio, who, though he no longer had to take the verbal thrashings of his old boss, admitted he sorely missed the cranky old man.

Thomas had taken a liking to Emilio and even helped him in the kitchen while the old

Portuguese chef told him fantastical stories of his youth, which the impressionable young boy reveled in. Sometimes the tales ended abruptly, and the old man always told Thomas he would continue the story on the morrow. Supposedly, they were true stories, but Emilio made most of them up. The boy did not know this, of course, nor did he care. As far as he was concerned, Emilio had fought alongside the Duke of Terceira at the Battle of Asseiceira, spiking an enemy cannon in the face of constant fire and being the hero of the day.

Emilio had prepared a feast for Isaac's return, with which Esther and Thomas, both assisted him. A Yankee pot roast with potatoes, carrots, onions, and peas. Thomas had overseen the biscuits, which he burned the first time, causing the kitchen to fill with smoke and making Emilio run hither and thither attempting to fan it out the open window. The second batch, however, with Esther's assistance, had turned out much better, though Thomas insisted on soaking the biscuits with plenty of warm butter. For dessert, Emilio had whipped up an apple pie for which Thomas got a scolding from both Esther and Emilio for sticking his fingers underneath the crust and scooping out some apple slices. However, after a humble apology, the boy was quickly forgiven for this juvenile indiscretion.

The feast began in earnest, with Isaac insisting Major Frost sit at the head of the table. The major, however, refused to budge, reasoning that this was now Isaac's house and he had earned the right to take the head seat by his gallant rescue of Joy. After arguing for several minutes, it was Joy who settled the matter. She whispered something into Thomas's ear and then, taking him by the hand, led him to the position of honor. This caused everyone present to burst into fits of laughter. Elijah even got in on the fun by folding his napkin into the shape of a crown and setting it on Thomas's curly head, which caused further merriment. Thomas was then asked to take a bow, which he performed with much dignity before he was tasked with saying grace. He bowed his head and folded his little hands in front of him.

"Dear Lord, I thank thee for all you have provided us. I thank thee for bringing back my big brother Isaac and my new sister Joy, and my new cousin Elijah and my new father the major, and even the snow that is falling, with which me and Isaac are going to build snowmen. I thank thee for everything. Dear Lord! In Jesus's name we pray, amen!"

The major gave a single clap. "Well said, young Thomas!"

Thomas, feeling proud of his accomplishment, smiled and repeated the major's clap, which caused another round of laughter.

The days after Isaac and Joy's arrival were not spent idly. The first order of business was to get Joy to the doctor. Her spells and headaches were becoming more frequent and the time between each one was decreasing. The doctor was the prominent surgeon that Esther had told Isaac about on the morning that they first met. He agreed to see Joy, but unfortunately, after a thorough examination, he confirmed what the doctor in Richmond had already told her. Her condition was almost certainly terminal. He prescribed her some laudanum for the pain but that was all he could do for her. Surgery was experimental and her symptoms told the doctor it would be a futile endeavor and prove fatal. Isaac was incensed. He had been under the impression that surgery was a possible option.

Isaac was more devastated by the news than Joy. She had learned to live with her condition and had now accepted the fact that she would soon die. She tried to cheer Isaac up, but the boy was not to be consoled. He sunk into a deep depression until one day out in the orchard he found Joy sitting under an apple tree. She was crying. When he asked her what was wrong, she told him that she was worried about him. It was then that he realized how selfish he had been. Here she was, with weeks or perhaps days left to live, and instead of complaining about her situation, she was thinking about him. It was selfless and he was ashamed of how he was reacting. It was now spring, and the big news was the attack on Fort Sumter and President Lincoln's call to arms. Isaac, however, could think of nothing else but Joy, and as they sat together under the tree, Joy reminded him about his promise.

"Isaac, you told me you would take me to see Bandy's pond. Can we go see it?"

Isaac had almost forgotten about that promise. He had not seen Bandy since he had left for Virginia five months earlier. Not that he did not want to see him. In fact, he thought of him often. However, he was so intent on finding a remedy for Joy's sickness that everything else seemed trivial to him. He was still not convinced something could not be done for her. He had written to doctors and even Harvard College for advice. It was almost always the same answer.

"Joy, we will go tomorrow. I...I apologize for my behavior, lately...but I am awfully unhappy."

The next morning Isaac told his driver, Byron, to prepare the carriage. Joy had been indisposed for most of the night but had recovered nicely by the time they set off. Isaac retraced the route that they had taken when he and Thomas first arrived in Boston. Only this time, he was going the other way.

Joy had dressed warmly, with a red shawl thrown over her bony shoulders. Isaac had noticed her change of appearance, her sunken cheeks with dark circles under her eyes, which seemed too large for her head. She had quit wearing her kerchief and had let her hair grow out. Her sister had braided it the evening before, and Isaac thought that she looked beautiful and told her so.

They soon left Boston behind them, with its noisy, bustling streets filled with vendors and newsboys calling out about the latest happenings in South Carolina. They passed the towering steeple of the old North Church and found themselves on the tree-lined road to Bandy's pond.

It was a quiet, reflective ride. They arrived early in the afternoon. It was a warm day, the sun reflecting off the goldenrod that flourished in the fields around the still water. There was a sweet odor of honeysuckle in the air and the daffodils were in full bloom. Isaac helped Joy from the carriage. She was having a hard time walking, and he took her arm and led her down the path toward the pond, leaving Byron with the carriage.

324

Craig R. Hipkins

A hummingbird flitted by them, searching for some sweet nectar at about the same time that a bullfrog leaped at their approach, causing ripples in the water. The slab of rock where Isaac had spent many days, and even nights, appeared before them and seemed to radiate in a white glow. It was a perfect spring day.

For a few seconds, Joy stood with her slender right hand shading her eyes from the sun. She peered out at the placid body of water she had heard so much about. Her lips quivered slightly as she pointed to the rock where Isaac had spent many contemplative hours.

"Can we sit?"

"Yes."

They sat down next to each other on the rock. He, sitting back on his elbows with his legs crossed, while she sat cross-legged. It was time to call Bandy. The boy whistled. It was his unique call that Bandy always responded to. Joy was watching him, her doe-like eyes worshiping his every move. To him, it was the same and as he whistled again, he set his gaze on her.

"Will he come?" she asked.

"He always comes."

He whistled for a third time and then a fourth, but Bandy did not appear. He swallowed hard and tried a fifth time and then a sixth. "Where...where is he?" he said fretfully. She could see him moistening his lips with his tongue. She knew all his nervous habits.

"He will come, Isaac. I know he will."

He was anxious, looking up at the trees behind him, expecting to see the familiar sight of his feathered friend, but nothing. Only a slight breeze stirring the bright green leaves of the poplars and maples. He stood up and was stricken with horror at the thought that something might have happened to Bandy.

"Bandy!" he called, desperately.

He whistled for the seventh and final time. That is when Joy saw him, while Isaac's back was turned, gliding off the branch of a sickly white pine leaning over the lake.

"Here he comes, Isaac!"

"Kehoo! Keehoo!"

The boy turned, his face beaming with happiness. He held up his hands and Bandy alighted on his shoulder pecking at his cheek affectionately.

"Bandy... Oh, how I missed you! It has been so long, my friend!"

He sat down and Joy leaned over and rubbed the pigeon's pink belly.

Bandy pecked at her hand, and she giggled. Isaac kissed the top of Bandy's head.

"Oh! Oh! Please tell me all about what has been happening at the pond while I have been away! How was the winter?" Isaac asked, beaming with happiness.

Bandy turned his head and seemed to ignore Isaac's question.

"Bandy? Did you hear me?"

The bird remained mute. His head turning from Isaac to Joy as if he might be deliberating who to address.

"Bandy?"

Isaac turned to Joy who had lowered her head with her chin resting on her chest.

"Bandy? Why won't you speak to me? Are you mad at me? Oh, I am sorry for not coming sooner, but I can explain——"

Joy placed a finger up to his lips and he stopped in mid-sentence, a perplexed look on his face.

"Isaac?"

He looked concerned. "Y—yeah?"

"He...he is not going to speak to you."

For a few seconds he was bewildered. His eyes blinking rapidly. Bandy tenderly pecking at his ear. "I...I don't understand. Why? Why won't he speak to me?"

She took his hand and held it. He did not need her to tell him, for he knew the truth but didn't want to admit it. Bandy had never spoken to him. It had all been in his mind. His desperate need for a friend had given him the illusion that the pigeon spoke to him, just as Joy, one time, long ago, thought the rabbit spoke to her.

"But why, Joy? Why?"

"You needed a friend, Isaac. And...and I needed a friend. Don't you see? You can't hear him now because you have me, and I have you. And...and you are growing up."

She rested her head on his chest, and he held her in his arms. He felt a tear run down his cheek and could hear her shallow breathing.

"Joy? You...you can't die, Joy. You just can't. You...you're my best friend. I love you, Joy. I...I don't know if I have the strength to continue..."

She tightened her feeble grip on his hand, and he reached over with his other hand and placed it on top of hers. A tear ran down her cheek as they looked into each other's eyes.

"You will continue, because you must. You have Thomas, Elijah, and Esther...and you will always have me, Isaac. My spirit will be with you always. It wasn't by accident that we met."

He kissed her on the cheek as he felt her weakening. He then saw her raise her finger toward the sky.

Suddenly, he perceived a low humming sound coming from the forest. It gradually became louder, until finally the trees came alive, seeming to burst forth from their trunks. However, it was only an illusion.

The pigeons came in droves, thousands of them, flapping their wings and crowding together in a tight mass. The sky slowly darkened as they blotted out the sun as if there were an eclipse, but nay, the darkness was only momentary. A small opening let the solar disk of the sun throw a wide beam on the rock below, shining its magnificence on the two youths, who were gazing up at the spectacle with amazement, feeling the glory of all that is good.

"Oh, look, Isaac! Look at the angels!"

And those were Joy's last words as Isaac felt her slip away from him. It was at that moment he knew she was right. She would always be with him. He smiled and cried. Bandy alighted from his shoulder and with Joy's soul in tow, led the procession as it turned into a great funnel and shot out and up into the heavens where all good things must one day go.

Finis

Craig R. Hipkins

A Note on the Passenger Pigeon

John J Audubon once observed a flock of pigeons he estimated to be over a billion in number. This was in 1813. One hundred years later the passenger pigeon was extinct.

Audubon described his 1813 encounter with this flock in the following way:

"I cannot describe to you the extreme beauty of their aerial evolutions, when a hawk chanced to press upon the rear of the flock. At once, like a torrent, and with a noise like thunder, they rushed into a compact mass, pressing upon each other towards the center. In these almost solid masses, they darted forward in undulating and angular lines, descended and swept close over the earth with inconceivable velocity, mounted perpendicularly so as to resemble a vast column, and, when high, were seen wheeling and twisting within their continued lines, which then resembled the coils of a gigantic serpent. Before sunset I reached Louisville, distant from

Hardensburgh fifty-five miles. The Pigeons were still passing in undiminished numbers and continued to do so for three days in succession. The people were all in arms. The banks of the Ohio were crowded with men and boys, incessantly shooting at the pilgrims, which there flew lower as they passed the river."

Audubon's description of this flock is amazingly descriptive. He also gives a hint of the doomed species fate at the end of the narrative. The passenger pigeon required nesting grounds that were being slowly destroyed by deforestation. This, along with excessive hunting sealed their unfortunate demise. The last passenger pigeon died in the Cincinnati Zoo in 1914. Her name was Martha.

Some great books on the passenger pigeon are Joel Greenberg's *A Feathered River Across the Sky* and John J. Audubon's *Ornithological Biography, or an Account of the Habits of the Birds of the United States of America*. An excellent book on

Craig R. Hipkins

deforestation and ecology is William Cronon's *Changes in the Land* which won the 1984 Francis Parkman Prize.